'Don't shut m.... here for you.'

She gave a low laugh. 'But for how long, Timothy? Soon you'll be up in Queensland with your underwater camera, snapping away at the reef.'

Soon he would be gone, out of her life and on to pastures new, and what then?

She'd always been independent, self-reliant, but Timothy had crept into her heart with alarming stealth, become the rock she leant on, her hope, her sounding board—and all too soon he was going to be taken away.

Of course she wanted him to stay—she wanted that more than anything else in the world—but she was terrified. Terrified of telling him just how much she wanted it.

Carol Marinelli is a nurse who loves writing. Or is she a writer who loves nursing? The truth is Carol's having trouble deciding at the moment, but writing definitely seems to be taking precedence! She's also happily married to an eternally patient husband and mother to three fabulously boisterous children. Add a would-be tennis player, an eternal romantic and a devout daydreamer to the list, and that pretty much sums Carol up. Oh, she's also terrible at housework!

Carol now also writes for Modern Romance™!

Recent titles by the same author:

Medical Romance™

THE BUSH DOCTOR'S CHALLENGE *
THE BABY EMERGENCY*
THE ELUSIVE CONSULTANT
THE SURGEON'S GIFT
EMERGENCY AT BAYSIDE

*Tennengarrah Clinic

THE DOCTOR'S OUTBACK BABY

BY
CAROL MARINELLI

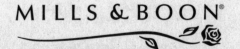

Helen, David, Ryan, William and Amy Browne,
with love.

First published in Great Britain 2004
Harlequin Mills & Boon Limited,
Eton House, 18-24 Paradise Road, Richmond, Surrey TW9 1SR

© Carol Marinelli 2004

ISBN 0 263 83890 0

Set in Times Roman 10½ on 12 pt.
03-0404-46595

Printed and bound in Spain
by Litografia Rosés, S.A., Barcelona

pealing. Even so, Clara blushed guiltily as she pressed the point, knowing her motives weren't entirely pure. 'I know she's a doctor, but we all pitch in with things like this, and she's not exactly enamoured of the place. I'm sure Abby wouldn't mind holding the fort.'

'I can't ask Abby.' Shelly shook her head, but an excited smile was starting to form on her lips as she looked around to check that the coast was clear. 'Honestly, Clara, I just can't.'

'What's going on?' Clara asked. 'Come on, Shelly, tell me. There's only Bill here and he's asleep. Why can't you ask Abby?'

'You have to promise not to breathe a word.' Shelly's eyes were wide. She was grinning broadly now and Clara found herself reluctantly smiling back, her annoyance with Shelly's thoughtlessness evaporating at the chance of a piece of gossip.

'I promise. Come on, Shelly, don't keep me in suspense. Has she finally decided to head off back to Sydney to her beloved emergency department?' Clara asked, rather too hopefully.

'Oh, it's better than that,' Shelly said excitedly, perching herself on the edge of the desk and beckoning Clara closer. 'And if you let it slip I'll never—'

'Get on with it.' Clara laughed, sitting back on her seat and waiting to hear what Shelly was so excited about.

'I can't ask Abby to work tonight, because I have it on excellent authority that someone else wants to ask her something.'

'I'm not with you.' Clara shook her head, bemused.

'You really don't have a clue, do you? Where have you been hiding the last week or so, Clara? The bush telegraph's been working overtime,' Shelly whispered excitedly. 'Guess where Kell is?'

'On a day off.'

'Yes, but guess what he's doing?'

'He said he was going into town,' Clara shrugged. 'Bruce was going to fly him there.'

'Which he did a couple of weeks ago, and Bruce saw him going into a jeweller's!' When Clara still didn't catch on Shelly thumped her playfully on the arm, jumping off the desk with an excited whoop as for Clara reality finally dawned. 'Kell's going to ask Abby to marry him, Clara! I'm on my way over to Abby's now. I've managed to squeeze her in to get her hair and nails done, though she's absolutely no idea what Kell's got planned. I can't possibly tell her that Bill's finally decided to have the op or she'll be over in a flash, that's why I'm bending over back-wards to sort out the roster and make sure everything goes smoothly. Nothing must spoil tonight for them. Can you believe Kell's actually going to propose?'

Clara couldn't.

For a moment the world stopped. She could hear Shelly laughing and talking in the background, was vaguely aware even of Ross and some other guy walking in, but for that moment in time her heart felt as if it wasn't beating any more. Clutching Bill's pile of notes to her chest as if it were some sort of shield, she sat there as the news washed over her.

Kell Bevan was going to propose.

After all these years Kell had finally got off his blue-jeaned backside and made a flight into town to pick up a ring on the day of the Tennengarrah ball.

It was just how she'd imagined it.

Just how she'd secretly dreamed it would be. The

barn alight with fairy-lights, tea-candles burning on the tables, the scent of white gardenias filling the night air, the stars twinkling endlessly above as Kell finally proposed.

Maybe she hadn't prayed hard enough.

Perhaps when she'd made the mental bargain with the powers that be she hadn't been specific enough, had forgotten to point out what should have been so blazingly obvious.

Kell should have been asking her.

CHAPTER ONE

'AND this is Clara, who knows more about Tennengarrah than the whole lot of us put together, don't you?'

'Sorry?' Realising that not only was she being spoken to but that a response was very much the order of the day, Clara turned her slightly startled expression to Ross.

'I was just telling Timothy here how much we all depend on you, and that if he needs anything he only has to ask.' Ross Bodey's rather strained smile left Clara in no doubt she'd been daydreaming too long and it hadn't gone unnoticed.

'He's the new doctor,' Shelly mumbled in an undertone, pushing Clara forward to shake Timothy's outstretched hand. 'From England.'

'But you're not due for a couple of weeks yet.'

It wasn't the most welcoming of greetings—in fact, on a rating of one to ten it would barely have scored—but, given the bombshell Shelly had just been dropped, Clara was amazed she could actually speak, and what was more her voice even sounded vaguely familiar!

'I ran out of cash.'

His admission startled her out of her confusion momentarily. Shifting the pile of notes into one arm, Clara accepted the outstretched hand and found herself looking into two smiling green eyes, even managing a rather forced smile back as thankfully he went over the formalities she had clearly missed.

'Timothy Morgan. It's a pleasure to meet you.'

'Clara Watts,' she mumbled, stealing a closer look. He certainly didn't look like someone who would run out of cash. His clothes, though casual, were certainly top notch and he had a very English, rather upper-crust accent, his thick curly brown hair was superbly cut but, more importantly, there was a slightly unassuming air about him, a refreshing openness to the smile he easily imparted as he shook her hand firmly. 'So you're from England. Are you here on a working holiday?'

'That's right,' Timothy answered cheerfully. 'Though I've been away for nearly a year now, working and trying to fit in all the touristy things.'

Lord, he could talk. She'd only asked a question to be polite! All Clara really wanted to do was dash off to the loo, bury her head in her hands and go over the news Shelly had so happily imparted. But instead she had to stand and make polite noises as Dr Timothy Morgan took her on an impromptu virtual tour of Australia, pulling photos out of his pocket like a magician as he told her how he'd bought a cheap ute, worked his way down the east coast of Australia and was now working his way up the middle.

'I was hoping to make my fortune in Coober Pedey,' Timothy chattered on easily. 'I read in my guide book that some tourists make enough to fund their entire trip, only in my case I spent three weeks fossicking in the dirt for opals and ended up spending a fortune having the two tiny stones I found mounted, which wasn't exactly the plan, so I'm hoping to start here early.'

'How early?' Shelly asked hopefully, peering at the roster as Ross started to laugh.

'You can't ask the poor guy to work on his first night here—he should be over at the ball, getting to know all the locals in one swoop. What's the problem?'

'I can't get anyone to work tonight.'

'But I thought Irene was coming.'

'She is, but she made it very clear she doesn't want to hand over to the Flying Doctors. So if they don't get here before seven, one of us is going to have to be here, and I can hardly ask Kell or Abby.'

'And you can't ask Clara,' Ross said firmly. 'She's on the ball committee, for goodness' sake, they've been planning this for months.'

'No, you can't ask Clara.'

The conversation that had been taking place ended abruptly, every eye turning as the new guy in town put in his ten cents' worth to a problem that clearly wasn't his.

'Because I intend to ask her to dance.'

It was an unfortunate moment to drop the pile of notes Clara had been precariously balancing.

Unfortunate, because from the look that flashed between Ross and Shelly they clearly thought Timothy's rather vocal intentions had caused her lapse in concentration.

Unfortunate, because Shelly, an eternal romantic at the best of times, would be for ever on her case now about the gorgeous new doctor and why didn't she make a bit of effort with him.

And unfortunate, because there was nothing dignified about scrabbling on the floor, trying to pick up endless reams of blood results and ECG printouts scattered over a seemingly ten-mile radius, with a heart that was bleeding inside.

Kell was going to propose.

It was like an awful mantra resounding in her head. Biting on her bottom lip to fight the sting of tears, Clara could feel her face reddening with the effort of not crying. She wished they'd all just leave her alone. Go and do whatever needed to be done on a Saturday morning and let her get on with her day.

Let her get on with her life.

A life without Kell.

'If the Flying Doctors haven't come by the time the balls starts, Irene can still watch him and give me a call when they get here. We'll hear the plane coming in anyway. It will only take half an hour or so to hand over.'

'But, Ross…' Shelly protested.

They were all on the floor, kneeling down and pretending not to notice Clara's red face and shaking hands.

'No buts,' Ross said firmly, standing up and shuffling the mass of papers into a pile that would take for ever to sort out. 'Have you told Bill's daughter the news?'

Clara shook her head, grateful for the change of subject. 'I've been ringing all morning but I can't get through.'

'No doubt she's out on the farm. It's probably best someone tells her face to face, given that she's pregnant and everything. I might head over now. Do you want to come, Timothy?'

'Where do they live?'

'Just out of town.'

Timothy gave a small grimace. 'Which in the outback means a couple of hours' drive. Sorry, Ross, would it be a terrible career move if I turned you down, given that I've just spent the last twenty-four hours bumping along in my ute to get here?'

'Of course not.' Ross laughed. 'I just feel guilty, leaving you on your own on your first morning here. Shelly's got a hairdresser's appointment, Kell and Abby are off duty…'

'I'll be fine,' Timothy said assuredly. 'A shower and a sleep are top of my list at the moment. Still…' those green eyes turned to Clara, who was attempting to fashion Bill's notes into some sort of order '…I wouldn't say no to a quick guided tour of the clinic, if Clara doesn't mind. I'd hate for something to happen and not have a clue where anything's kept.'

'Good idea,' Ross said enthusiastically, obviously thrilled to have Timothy on board. 'You don't mind, do you, Clara?'

There it was again, the automatic assumption that she'd come good. 'You don't mind' was up there with 'I hate to ask' and Clara's personal favourite, 'Oh, Clara will do it'.

Well, she did mind.

Right now she wanted some peace, wanted to sort out Bill's notes, wanted some time to gather her thoughts and figure out what on earth she was going to do, not hold yet another new doctor's hand and show another fleeting visitor the ropes, only to have them leave again.

Of course she didn't say as much. Instead, she nodded, her clear blue eyes briefly meeting Timothy's. 'Sure, I'd be happy to.'

'Great.'

*　　*　　*

'Sorry about this,' Timothy ventured once they were alone. 'I'm sure you've got a million and one things to do without taking me around. It's just that I went for an interview at a bush hospital up in Queensland when I first came to Australia. I got there early, as you do for interviews, and a patient went and had a cardiac arrest while I was sitting outside the interview room.'

Clara was only half listening as she pushed open the coffee-room doors and pointed in the vague direction of the staff kitchen before heading towards the main work area. Timothy's backpacking stories really held no interest for her.

'Anyway, it turns out I was so early the doctor interviewing me wasn't in the hospital yet.'

'Really?' Clara said distractedly, turning up the volume on Bill's cardiac monitor before she crossed the room as Timothy hovered annoyingly over her right shoulder, watching her every move. 'I'll take you though to our treatment room.'

'So there I was, going over my interview technique, the ink on my medical certificate barely dry, and this nurse came running up.'

'Two beds,' Clara said, pushing open the heavy back swing doors as Timothy carried on nattering. 'This sometimes doubles as a second resuscitation area if we get a major incident...' Her voice trailed off in mid-sentence and she turned around sharply. 'You were the only doctor in the hospital?'

'Barely a doctor, really.' Timothy nodded as Clara's mouth fell open. 'I came to Australia as soon as I finished med school—I hadn't even had my new cheque books delivered.' He watched a frown pucker her freckled face. 'One of life's better moments.'

Timothy smiled. 'Ringing up the bank and asking them to change the Mr to Dr. You'd be amazed how that surly voice on the other end of the phone changes when they realise your rather shaky bank balance is in for some serious improvement.'

'But you're too...' Snapping her mouth closed, Clara didn't finish her sentence, but Timothy had already got the gist.

'Too old to be an intern?' he finished for her with a grin. 'I was a mature student. In fact, a student's practically all I've ever been. I spent three years at uni fiddling around doing a business and finance degree, then two months out in the big wide world made me realise the family business just wasn't for me. They're financial planners.' Timothy grimaced. 'My parents get the same thrill watching the stock market that I get watching a cardiac monitor.'

Clara laughed, actually laughed. 'Sounds as if you could use some financial planning yourself.'

But Timothy just shook his head. 'Heaven forbid. Sure, I could ring them up and ask them to wire me some money but I wouldn't give them the satisfaction.' He gave a grim smile. 'There's the rest of my life to worry about mortgage payments and retirement funds. When I get back to England I'm hoping to study to become a surgeon so there's years of being sensible ahead, but for now I intend to enjoy myself, despite my parents' objections.'

Clara sensed the edge of his voice but chose not to push. 'So what happened?' She registered his frown. 'At your interview in Queensland?'

'Oh, that!' Timothy grinned, his easy smile back in place now. 'Well, this nurse comes rushing up and tells me that Mr Forbes in bed four has gone into a cardiac arrest.'

'So what did you do?' There was impatience to her voice, which Timothy seemed not to notice.

'Well, for starters I asked just where bed four was, and while she was at it would she mind telling me who the hell Mr Forbes was and, perhaps more pointedly, if there was another doctor in the house.'

'But what did you do with the patient?' Clara pushed, genuinely enthralled now, as any nurse would have been at such a story. 'What on earth happened?'

'I took a crash course in crash calls.' He laughed. 'Thank heavens I watch *ER*. I was giving out orders, calling out to charge the defibrillator, massaging Mr Forbes's chest. I even intubated him.'

'Really?' Clara asked, suitably impressed, but Timothy shrugged modestly.

'I'd had a few goes in Theatre.'

'But still,' Clara enthused. 'There's a big difference between the controlled setting of Theatre with an anaesthetist over your shoulder and running your first cardiac arrest on your own. You did really well.'

'Not that well,' Timothy groaned. 'The patient died.'

'Ouch.'

'And I didn't get the job.'

'But why?' Clara protested. 'That's so unfair.'

'That's life.' Timothy shrugged. 'Someone smarter, with more experience, got in first.'

'I know the feeling,' Clara muttered.

'Sorry?'

'It doesn't matter. Come on, I'll show you around properly, though hopefully there won't be any repeats.' They walked around the theatre, Clara point-

ing things out, flicking machines on and off and taking Timothy through the resuscitation trolley, even
surprising herself by pursuing a conversation with
him.

'So, which hospital did you end up in?'

'Adelaide.'

'But that's the other end of the country,' Clara
pointed out.

'And I took my time getting there, let me tell you.'

'Maybe later.' Clara grinned. 'I do actually have
some work to do.'

'Sorry, I tend to go on a bit, but despite my poverty
I've just about saved up enough money to head back
to Queensland when I'm finished here and do the next
level diving course.'

'You've already done one?'

'Two,' Timothy replied. 'It was amazing. You
should see some of the photos I've taken of the barrier
reef—I'll show you some time. Have you been there?'

Clara shook her head. 'I haven't been anywhere.
Apart from three years in Adelaide to study nursing,
I've never been away from here. It sounds wonderful,
though. I've heard it's stunning.'

'Oh, it is and nothing beats seeing it at first hand.
Our diving instructor gave us some food to take
down. The fish actually come and feed out of your
hands—I even saw a shark not six feet away.'

'Don't,' Clara yelped. 'I'd die.'

'I nearly did,' Timothy responded, his eyes widening in fear just at the memory. 'Apparently if you
ignore them they'll ignore you, but I must have used
up half my air tank I was hyperventilating so much.
You should do it some day, take off and backpack

around this amazing land. It's been the best year of my life.'

'I'd love to,' Clara admitted, 'but I can't see it happening. I can barely get a night off to go to the ball. Can you imagine Ross and Shelly if I asked for a whole year?'

'Don't ask.' Timothy shrugged. 'Just do it.'

'Easier said than done.' Looking up, she realised Timothy was waiting for her to elaborate. 'The clinic used to be tiny, just one room and one theatre, when I started. But since Ross and Shelly came last year it's really grown. Ross is totally committed to the place, he's for ever lobbying for more staff and more funds and for the most part it's worked. The closed-off area is yet another extension and when that's completed we're going to be upgraded from a clinic to a bush hospital. There's going to be two wards and a proper delivery suite, which will be great, of course, but the trouble is the staff ratio hasn't exactly kept up with the patients so far. Kell and I do most of it between us, Shelly pitches in when she can, but she's got a new baby and a three-year-old to take care of. She wants to be at home with her babies and, frankly, I don't blame her. Matthew, her three-year-old, has got Down's syndrome,' Clara explained, but Timothy just nodded.

'I know.'

'So her hands are full already, without taking on a load of extra shifts.'

'So it all falls on you?'

'And Kell,' Clara said quickly, but when Timothy just stared back at her she let out a low sigh. 'Mainly me at the moment,' she admitted. They were in the storeroom now, out of earshot of Bill, so Clara was able to be honest. 'We don't normally have inpatients, at least not for more than a couple of nights, but Bill didn't want to be transferred and he was too sick to go home…'

'And, of course, Kell was busy with Abby,' Timothy said perceptively. 'So it all came down to you. You are allowed to have a life, too, you know.'

'It's not that bad,' Clara protested. 'It's just been a bit full on these past few weeks.'

'You should take some time off, I bet you've got heaps owing. Go and see this magical land of yours. I know that's what I'll be doing once I've done my three-month stint here. When I've got my advanced diver's certificate I'll be able to take tourists out to the reef myself. I've got a two-year working holiday visa and I intend to use every last day of it. Diving's great.'

'There's not much ocean in Tennengarrah,' Clara needlessly pointed out.

'Then I'll just have to stick to medicine while I'm here, I guess.' He was smiling at her and, what was more amazing given her mood only twenty minutes earlier, Clara was smiling back, only this time it wasn't forced or awkward. This time it seemed the most natural thing in the world. 'Thanks for the tour and by the way…' He was walking out now, heading for the door as Clara turned back to Bill's notes. 'I still want that dance.'

'So Cinderella shall go to the ball after all.'

The sound of Bill's voice filling the silence made Clara jump. Crossing the room, she smiled at her patient as she wrapped the blood-pressure cuff around his arm.

'You were supposed to be asleep.'

'Everyone would have stopped talking if I'd opened my eyes. It's nice to hear a bit of a gossip.'

Bill had been lying in a state of lethargic depression for weeks now, and Clara was so relieved to see his familiar, kind eyes with a bit of sparkle back in them that her own worries flew out of the window. After checking his obs, she perched on the edge of his bed for a little chat.

'It's good to have you back, Bill.'

'It's good to be back. Now that I've finally decided to go ahead and have the bypass I feel better.'

'You'll feel even better when you've had the operation. Not at first, of course, but after a month or two you'll be a new man, Bill. I'm sure you've made the right choice.'

'I hope so.' She could see the glimmer of fear in his eyes and instinctively Clara put her hand over his and gave it a small squeeze. 'You're a good girl, Clara,' Bill said as he gripped her hand back. 'Ross, Kell, Shelly, Abby, they're all great and everything, but you're one in a million, do you know that?'

'Stop getting maudlin.' Clara blushed, but Bill wouldn't let up.

'I remember when your parents died. One of Tennengarrah's blackest days it was. We were all so worried about you, wondering what would become of you. Just fifteen years old and with no one to take care of you…'

'I had loads of people,' Clara broke in. 'Everyone helped.'

'Still, a lot of fifteen-year-olds would have gone off the rails. But not you. You put your head down and got on with it, didn't you? Really made something of yourself. The whole town's so proud of you, Clara. You're a true Tennengarrah girl.'

'So is Kell,' Clara pointed out, trying not to linger on his name too long, trying to have a normal conversation without betraying the agony in her heart. It wasn't too hard to do. After all, she'd been hiding her feelings where Kell was concerned for years, it came almost as naturally as breathing. 'He's a guy, of course, but he's a local, too.'

'For how long, though?'

On any other day and under any other circumstance she'd have managed a shrug or a smile, managed to carry on talking as if she didn't have a care in the world, as if Kell Bevan was just another friend and colleague. Only today she couldn't do it.

Today as Clara sat in the still, quiet ward with her one and only patient, something that felt suspiciously like a tear pricked her eye as Bill carried on talking.

'This is hard on you, isn't it, Clara?'

'What do you mean?' Confused, she shook her head, went to pull her hand away, but Bill gripped it tighter and those kind eyes stared back at her thoughtfully.

'Kell's a bit more than just a friend to you, isn't he?'

Aghast, Clara's eyes widened, her mouth opening to let out a small wail of protest, but Bill moved quickly to reassure her.

'No one knows, so don't be embarrassed. I've known you all your life, you're like a second daughter to me, but even I didn't have a clue. You've always just been Kell and Clara, two school kids, two mates and later two nurses. I never even realised until a couple of weeks ago how you felt. But watching the two of you working together, how your whole face lights up when he comes in the room, how difficult it's been for you when Abby's around, well, I guess something just clicked in my head. You do care for him, don't you?'

It was pointless denying it, pointless when tears were streaming down her face as her old mate Bill gently held her hand.

Bill wasn't just a patient—he was friend, a surrogate uncle. Endless nights had been spent in the cosy womb of his kitchen after her parents had died. Bill and his beloved wife had taken her under their wing, the whole town had, in fact, ensuring she'd always felt loved. Cheering her on through her school exams then later welcoming her back with open arms when finally she'd got her nursing degree.

Lying to Bill wasn't an option.

'I was going to tell him how I felt tonight,' Clara whispered. 'I knew he was seeing Abby, but I really didn't think it was that serious. I thought she was just another girlfriend, that she'd move on in a couple of weeks and things would be back to normal, and now it would seem that they're getting engaged.'

'She hasn't said yes yet,' Bill pointed out.

'Oh, she will,' Clara said ruefully. 'And deep down I know that it's right. They love each other, they're really well suited. It's just so hard to take it all in…'

'Oh, Clara.' Bill lay back on his pillow as she struggled to hold it together.

'I'm sorry, Bill, I'm supposed to be cheering you up, not landing all of this on you.'

'I wouldn't have it any other way,' Bill said gently. 'Things will get better for you Clara. When my Raelene died I thought my life was over. I never thought I'd be happy again, didn't care if I lived or died. And now look at me. I've got a grandchild on the way, I'm having an operation that will give me another decade. And you know what? I reckon once this op is over, once I'm back home, on a good day I'll even be able to say that I'm truly happy, and you'll be able to say it one day, too. It won't always hurt this much.'

'I know,' Clara said bravely, then changed her mind. 'Actually, I don't know, but I really hope so, Bill.'

'Hey, there's plenty more fish in the sea…'

'Bill…' Clara let out a rueful laugh. 'As I just said to Timothy, there's no ocean for miles here, there's really not that many fish to choose from in Tennengarrah.'

'What about the *Carry On* guy?'

'Who?'

'*Carry On Doctor*, the one with the posh voice who killed his first patient.'

'What are you talking about?'

'The one he was talking about—the guy who had the heart attack at his interview in Queensland! Like I said, I was only pretending to be asleep.'

'He didn't kill him, Bill.' Clara grinned through her tears. 'It wasn't Timothy's fault he couldn't save him—it actually sounds as if he did really well. There's not many junior doctors that could intubate a patient under those sorts of circumstances. At least the patient was given every chance.'

'I guess.' Bill gave Clara a small wink. 'I had a quick peek when he came in and he's a good-looking guy, that Timothy.'

'Don't go there, Bill,' Clara warned, but he carried on anyway.

'Why ever not? He's already lined you up for a dance. Maybe tonight won't be such a disaster after all.'

'Forget it. Tonight's already a disaster.' Standing up, Clara gave her favourite patient the benefit of a very nice smile. 'How about a cuppa?

'And some toast and Vegemite?' Bill asked hopefully. 'I'm not nil by mouth yet.'

'Give me ten minutes to sort out your notes and I'll make us both a round of toast. I could use some comfort food right now,' Clara said warmly, thrilled that Bill's appetite was finally returning.

And not just his appetite, Clara realised happily. Bill was flicking through the TV guide with more than passing interest.

'There's your favourite soap opera starting soon, Clara. Why don't you pull up a chair and have your lunch-break here? I promise not to mention Kell.'

'It's a deal.' Heading for the desk, Clara turned briefly, back in control now but still just a little shy at having finally revealed her secret. 'You come back to us safe, Bill.'

'I hope so.'

'I know so.'

CHAPTER TWO

BECAUSE it didn't matter any more, because it mattered not a jot how well she did her make-up or how well her fine red hair behaved, tonight of all nights everything worked.

The subtle blonde foils Clara had reluctantly agreed to at Anna the hairdresser's insistence lifted her short, practical hairstyle into a pretty gamine crop, accentuating her clear blue eyes and high freckled cheekbones. She hadn't used the green foundation, though. She'd had it in her drawer for weeks, had bought it on an occasional trip to town, won over by the sophisticated shop assistant who'd sworn it would neutralise even the deepest blush.

Oh, and how she would have blushed.

Blinking back a fresh crop of tears, Clara tried to beat back the image of finally telling Kell how she felt. How she'd planned to take him outside, away from Abby, away from the prying eyes of the locals, and tell him that he wasn't or ever had been just a friend…

Shaking her head firmly, Clara took a deep breath, refusing to go down that track, refusing to indulge herself in wasted dreams. Instead, she eyed herself critically in the mirror, pleased despite herself with her efforts. Even the rather shakily applied mascara and neutral lipstick for once didn't look like a little girl had practised with her mother's make-up. The antithesis of vain, she didn't even possess a full-length mirror, so the only way to view her dress was by standing precariously on the toilet lid, which, Clara realised, didn't really give the full effect when your head was chopped off from view.

Oh, lord!

Swallowing nervously, she stared at the sleek black-stockinged legs that seemed to go on for ever, a massive expanse of unfamiliar thigh slimmed down by the high heels she was wearing, but even the occasional appearance of her legs didn't jolt her as much as the sight of her breasts, jacked up in a strapless bra, wriggling and jumping in excitement at their first taste of freedom from her practical sports bra.

It was too much, way, way too much! Everyone would fall off their chairs laughing when she walked in.

Glancing at her watch, Clara bit back a surge of panic. It was already ten past seven, she was supposed to be setting up the food table now, the band would be waiting for their pay cheque before they started and if she didn't go now…

Picking up a massive tray of egg and chutney sandwiches, Clara headed for the door, then changed her mind midway. Dumping the tray in the hallway, she dashed back into her bedroom and drenched herself in perfume, then ran around the house in a manic frenzy, trying to remove every lingering trace of the beastly three dozen eggs she'd hard-boiled before heading outside and walking down the high street towards the barn and wondering why the hell she'd even bothered.

She'd be coming home alone.

Nobody laughed.

Oh, there were a few whistles and cat calls when

she walked in, blushing furiously and wishing she wasn't carrying a pile of sandwiches so she could hitch down her dress a bit, and a couple of the guys slapped her on the back as if they were bringing up her wind and reminded Clara that if she had any trouble tonight she only had to ask.

As if she'd run into any trouble, Clara sighed, adding her tray to the heaving table. As if she was going to have to beat off a stream of admirers with a stick.

'You look fabulous, Clara!' Shelly made a beeline for her. 'Your dress is divine, you look just wonderful.'

'So do you.' Clara smiled. 'Where's Ross?'

'I was about to ask you the same. He "popped" over to the clinic an hour ago. You didn't see the Flying Doctors' plane there when you went past by any chance?'

Clara shook her head. 'He's probably just writing up the transfer letter. Bill's case is pretty complicated.' The frown on Shelly's face told Clara she wasn't appeased. 'He'll be here soon. Anyway, the night's still young, the band's booked until one—speaking of which, I'd better go and pay them.'

'Well, hurry back,' Shelly whispered loudly. 'There's no Ross, no Kell and no Abby. Even Timothy hasn't made his way over. Apart from me and the kids, our table's the emptiest one in the barn.'

She would have hurried back—in fact, Clara would have loved to have sat down and had a glass of punch or champagne, but instead Hamo, Jim and Mitch all decided to get their duty dances out of the way early and the next twenty minutes or so were spent being twirled around the floor by various colours of checked shirts as the band sang about shearing sheep, billy tea and all the things Australians held dear after a few cans of beer. Arriving back at the table, her face flushed, giggling at one of Hamo's more lewd jokes, her smile instantly faded as several strained faces turned to greet her.

'What's wrong?'

'Nothing,' Ross said too brightly.

'Where's Abby?'

'The Flying Doctors came,' Kell replied, without looking up. 'They needed a doctor escort.'

'Why?' Clara asked immediately. The Flying Doctors were exactly that, and Bill wasn't that sick at the moment. She couldn't think of one possible reason why Abby would have needed to go. 'Who was the doctor?'

'Hall Jells. He just thought it would be safer if the clinic provided an escort,' Ross responded, without meeting her eyes, and from the pained look Shelly was flashing at her Clara decided not to pursue it, instead taking a glass of champagne from Bruce, the local pilot who was doubling as a waiter, and trying to ignore just how divine Kell looked tonight.

'So this is where all the action is.' The appearance of Timothy lifted the mood somewhat. Everyone fell on him as if he were a long-lost friend, obviously grateful for the diversion, and Clara found herself frowning. She felt as if she'd turned on her favourite soap only to realise she'd missed an important episode. Everyone was talking normally, smiling and cheerful, but something wasn't right.

Something was definitely going on.

'I fell asleep,' Timothy explained needlessly, and, choosing the chair next to Clara's, he sat down and gave her the benefit of a very nice smile. 'It was supposed to be a fifteen-minute power nap.' He glanced at his watch. 'But that was about four hours ago.'

'Well, I'm glad you made it.' It was merely a polite comment, just as she would have given to any newcomer, but Timothy caught her eye and suddenly the massive barn seemed to shrink.

'Really?' Timothy asked, as if it really mattered.

Taking a nervous sip of her champagne, Clara held it in her mouth for a second or two before swallowing, wishing she had used that blessed green foundation after all.

'Really,' she said finally, the admission surprising even herself.

Clean-shaven and freshly showered, Timothy was pretty easy on the eye, but it wasn't just his undeniable good looks that were working their charm here. There was something about his smile that told Clara it was just for her.

'You look wonderful,' Timothy said very slowly and very deliberately, and for all the world he sounded as if he really meant it. 'Your hair looks nice, different.' Green eyes raked over her and Clara could feel her pulse flickering in her neck as he scrutinised her slowly.

'I—I had foils,' she stammered. 'Just a couple…'

'I've no idea what foils are.' Timothy grinned.

'A few blonde tips.'

Timothy nodded. 'Looks great, although I love red hair.'

'That's because you haven't got red hair,' Clara countered, blushing ever deeper. And even though the conversation flowed easily, even though they were only talking about foils and hair and oversleeping, she felt as if she were caught in a rip, seemingly following the tide of a normal conversation as a throbbing undercurrent pulled her in an opposite, unfamiliar and definitely dangerous direction.

'I'll go and get another round. Clara, do you want to give me a hand?' Kell asked, standing up. Instead of falling over her chair to help him as was usually the case, for the first time in living memory, Kell actually had to repeat himself as she laughed at something Timothy had said. 'Clara, do you want to give me a hand with the drinks?'

'I'm fine.' Clara smiled, deliberately missing the point, gesturing to her half-full glass as Kell shrugged and turned to go.

'I'll help!' Matthew jumped up, determined to impress his big buddy Kell. 'We can play—'

'Hide and seek,' Kell groaned, but his face broke into a smile as he took little Matthew's hand. 'We'll have one more game of hide and seek and then I'll get that beer.'

'How about that dance?' Timothy pushed, but Clara shook her head, turning briefly to check Kell really was out of earshot.

'How about someone telling me what's going on,' Clara said sharply to her friends gathered around the table. 'Why on earth has Abby gone to Adelaide as a doctor escort?'

'Tell her, Ross,' Shelly choked, her voice unusually angry. 'Tell Clara the mess you've made of things.'

Clara almost spilt her drink in surprise. Never in all the time she's known Shelly and Ross had they been anything other than devoted to each other. She'd never heard so much as a cross word pass between them and now here they were practically rowing at the table in front of everyone. Something was wrong, seriously wrong, and Clara stared from one to the other with her mouth gaping open.

'Come on, Ross!' Timothy grinned eagerly and then shut up when every one turned and shushed him.

'Abby's gone,' Ross started slowly, as Clara's mouth dropped ever further. 'She's leaving tonight with the Flying Doctors. She found out Kell was going to propose and she simply couldn't face it. She didn't want to leave like this, but on the other hand she didn't know how to say goodbye.'

'Does Kell know?' Clara's voice was barely a croak. She wished she'd used the green foundation now. Her face must surely be as red as a beetroot as she struggled with the news, relief flooding her veins intermingled with a horrible surge of guilt as she glanced over to the bar where Kell stood.

'No!' It was Shelly speaking now, the bitterness in her voice clearly evident. 'Ross is going to tell him that little gem later, once the ball's over, though I'm sure he knows something's up. The poor guy's walking around with an engagement ring in his pocket and he doesn't even know that Abby's bolted!' She turned her teary face to her husband. 'Well, you can leave me out of it, Ross. I just can't bear to see his face when you tell him what you've done.'

'I didn't do anything,' Ross said through gritted teeth. 'You were the one who had to go and spill the beans to Abby. If you'd just stayed out of it we wouldn't be in this mess.'

'So it's my fault now.'

'It isn't anyone's fault,' Ross relented, putting a hand over Shelly's. 'It's just the way things have turned out. Abby didn't want to hurt Kell when she said no. She was beside herself and she didn't know what else to do.'

'But why?' Clara asked, utterly bemused that any-one could run out on Kell. 'Why would she leave when he was going to propose and everything?'

'She just couldn't deal with it,' Ross said, tight-lipped. 'She belongs in the city—'

'He's coming back,' Timothy interrupted, 'so now might be a good time to change the subject.'

An awful silence followed as every one struggled to come up with something, until the baleful eyes that had silenced Timothy earlier begged him for help as Kell returned with a tray of beers.

'We have pints in England!' Timothy started, and Clara groaned into her wine at his dreadful efforts at conversation, but, as it turned out, Timothy was spot on. A lengthy discussion ensued between Kell and Timothy on the merits of pints versus schooners, warm versus icy cold and the alcohol content of ei-ther, giving the collective table enough time to exhale their held breaths and at least look as if a bombshell hadn't been dropped.

It was a great evening.

People often wonder what committees do, how one little ball could take so many months of preparation. But all their work, all the painstaking attention to de-tail paid off a hundredfold as midnight struck and the lights dimmed a further notch, the bush music slow-ing to love ballads matching the mellower mood of the crowd.

'What's going on, Clara?' Kell mumbled into his beer. 'The Flying Doctors wouldn't have needed an escort for Bill—you know that as well as I do. I've been trying to get you on your own all night to find out what's happening. Please, Clara, I need to know.'

Blinking rapidly, trying to choose her words carefully, Clara put a tentative hand across the table, opening her mouth to speak and praying she'd say the right thing.

'Time for that dance, I think.' Never had Timothy's timing been more appalling. Turning her angry eyes to him, she shook her head.

'Not now, Timothy,' she said, the irritation in her voice evident. Couldn't he see this was a private conversation?

'No excuses,' Timothy responded cheerfully, pulling her reluctantly to her feet as Clara turned and gave an apologetic shrug to Kell.

'Hold on a second.' Making her way back to the table, ignoring Timothy's obvious impatience, she met Kell's eyes. 'I'll speak to you outside after this dance.'

'What was that about?' Timothy asked once they were on the dance floor.

'Nothing.' Clara shrugged, grateful the dance floor was so packed and she could bury her flaming cheeks in Timothy's chest. She really was a useless liar.

'Because it really wouldn't be very sensible to tell Kell tonight.'

Startled, she looked up, surprised that he knew her secret.

'It would probably sound better coming from Ross.'

Relief flooded her veins, pleased that he didn't know her ulterior motives, but her relief was short-lived, turning instead into anger. She damned well wasn't about to take advice from Timothy, he hadn't even been in Tennengarrah a night yet. As if he knew what was best for Kell!

'Just leave it, Timothy,' she snapped. 'You don't know all that's gone on.'

'Keep your hair on.'

Rolling her eyes, Clara prayed the music would stop. OK, he was good-looking, funny at times and, yes, she admitted reluctantly he was a great dancer, but she hadn't heard the saying 'keep your hair on' since high school and she certainly wasn't going to let this overgrown teenager thwart her one stab at happiness tonight.

Abby had gone. Kell was devastated.

Why shouldn't he hear the news from someone who cared?

'Looks like they've made up,' Timothy commented as Ross and Shelly floated by. Shelly's eyes closed as she rested her head on Ross's shoulder, a dreamy smile on her face as they drifted along out of time with the music.

'It's the first time I've heard a cross word between them,' Clara admitted. 'Mind you, Shelly was pretty excited about tonight, she wants the world to be as happy in love as she is.'

'That's a nice thing to want.'

Clara didn't respond. Instead, she leant against Timothy, letting him lead, and perhaps for the first time that night she actually relaxed and enjoyed the fruits of the nine months of preparation that the ball had taken as she ambled along in time with the music, just enjoying the moment, enjoying the heavy throb of the bass and even revelling for a moment in the delicious spicy spell of his aftershave.

Timothy really was a good dancer, she thought almost reluctantly as the music stopped and they stood apart.

'I love this song.' Timothy smiled as the band started up again. 'Can I persuade you to join me for a second dance?'

Clara hesitated. She loved this song, too, and if truth be known she'd actually enjoyed dancing with Timothy. It hadn't been awkward like it was with some of the guys, hadn't been the duty dance every man in Tennengarrah felt compelled to have with the trusty Clara. Timothy had actually made her feel like a woman, not some annoying little sister, but she'd promised to meet Kell.

'Better not,' Clara said, the reluctance in her voice surprising even herself. 'But thanks, that was nice.'

Making her way across the room, she longed to dart into the toilet, desperate to check that she looked OK, to be sure she looked her best for the most difficult conversation of her life.

Gulping the night air into her lungs, she stared out into the darkness. The throb of music coming from the barn sounded a mile away as she stared up at the twinkling stars and begged for inspiration, her heart rate rising alarmingly as she heard heavy footsteps. Turning expectantly, forcing a smile, she stared into the darkness as he approached, not quite ready but determined not to miss her moment.

'Timothy!' The shock in her voice was evident. 'What are you doing here?'

'Getting some fresh air.' He shrugged. 'The same as you.'

Clara raked her mind. She didn't want to be rude, didn't want to be obvious, and she definitely didn't want to explain to Timothy why it was so important he left right now, but really he was leaving her with very little choice.

'Please, Timothy,' she started, her eyes turning frantically to the barn, her ears straining at the sound of approaching footsteps that she knew this time were definitely Kell's. 'I really need you to go.'

'Why?'

'I just do,' Clara whispered loudly. 'I really need to be on my own right now.'

'No, you don't.'

Aghast, she watched as he folded his arms and eyed her thoughtfully.

'In fact, I'd say the best thing you could do right now is get yourself inside and have that other dance with me.'

'Timothy, please, you don't understand...' she begged.

'Oh, but I do,' Timothy replied, and for the first time since she'd met him his voice was serious and there wasn't a glimmer of humour in his green eyes. 'You like Kell, don't you?'

'Of course I like Kell,' Clara spluttered. 'I've known him for—'

'I don't mean as a friend, Clara. You like Kell and you're hoping that when you tell him about Abby, he's going to realise just how much he actually likes you!'

Her shocked expression only confirmed his diagnosis.

'You're looking at a guy whose best friend was the captain of the rugby team,' he offered by way of explanation. 'I've spent more time than I care to remember watching other people's relationships flourish from the sidelines of my beer glass.'

'You've got it all wrong,' Clara insisted. Kell was practically on top of them. Any moment now he'd see them together and she needed to be alone for this.

'I don't think so,' Timothy responded, moving forward. 'Now, I'm going to apologise in advance for what I'm about to do, and though you probably won't realise it now, though you're probably going to hate me for it, I'm about to stop you from making the biggest mistake of your life.'

'What on earth—?'

She didn't get to finish, didn't get to say another word. Suddenly a hot wedge of flesh was pressing against her, pinning her up against the barn wall as she struggled furiously, her automatic scream hushed by the weight of his lips, her arms clamped against his chest with absolutely no room for manoeuvre.

Yet for all the shock, for all the adrenaline pumping through her veins, fear didn't enter into it. She knew Timothy's infuriating intentions, knew the sight of her stockinged legs hadn't catapulted him into a sexual frenzy. This was a duty kiss, she realised as she wrestled to get away, a duty kiss of the worst possible magnitude. And worse, far worse, despite struggling like a cat being dipped in water, despite her internal fury at her misdirected assailant, for the tiniest second, for a smidgen of time so small it was barely there, the fighting stopped, the resistance in her slipping away as other, rather more disturbing thoughts flitted into her mind.

Irrational thoughts that really shouldn't be given any credence…

The tangy aftershave that had assailed her on the dance floor, stronger now at such close proximity, his heavy ragged breathing as his chest moved against hers, the feel of her breasts pushed against the cool cotton of his shirt, and the faint tang of whisky as his lips moved against hers.

'Clara?' She could hear Kell's voice in the darkness, hear him closing in on them, and she made a last agonised struggle to escape. But Timothy was having none of it, his grip tightening on her more, if that was possible, as Kell approached.

'Oh!' She heard the surprise in Kell's voice, the muffled cough as he backed away. 'Sorry, guys.'

Only when Kell had gone, only when he was sure they were alone did Timothy pull away, his arms on the wall either side of her now like a temporary cage as he met her furious, glittering eyes.

'How dare you?' she started, her voice breathless, legs trembling with fury and something else that she would have died before admitting to. A great kisser he might be but she certainly wasn't going to let this over-inflated, pompous Englishman know that two minutes up close and personal with him had had the slightest effect in the romance stakes. She was furious.

That was all.

'How dare you?' she repeated, her voice a touch stronger now but no match for Timothy who broke in before she could even get started.

'Tonight's not the night, Clara. It's better coming from Ross.'

She shook her head incredulously, straightening up but still no match for his height even in her stilettos. 'How would you know? You haven't even been here a full day and you think you know what Kell needs. What, is it better coming from a guy? Better that a doctor breaks the news?'

Timothy shook his head, opening his mouth to speak, but nothing was stopping Clara now. Her voice finally found, she let it rip.

'Ross has only been here a year. I've known Kell all my life, so I don't need Ross to tell me when I can and can't talk to a friend, and I most certainly don't need to hear it from you. He has every right to know, every right to hear it—'

'I agree.'

'You do?' Confused, her voice stalled momentarily, the fire dying in her voice as she turned her questioning eyes to him.

'Of course he should know about Abby, but that's all. You can deny it all you like, but I'm sure there was more you were going to tell him and kissing you was the only thing I could think of to stop you from making the biggest mistake of your life.' Her burning anger was replaced with scorching shame, the glittering, defiant eyes sparkling with embarrassed tears as Timothy carried on gently, even smoothing a stray tendril of hair back behind her ear as she stood there, mortified.

'And if you told Kell you loved him, that's exactly what it would have been.'

'Hey, Clara, is everything all right?'

Hamo's none-too-dulcet tones made them both jump, Clara because she wasn't expecting it and Timothy because from the look on Hamo's face anything other than a positive reply wasn't going to be pretty.

She could have said no, could have burst into tears and landed Timothy right in it, but instead she forced a bright voice as the heavy weight approached. 'Everything's fine, Hamo.'

'You're sure?' he checked, eyeing Timothy in anything other than a friendly fashion. 'Because if you need anything you only have to give us a call.'

'I'm fine, Hamo, really.'

They both stood in strained silence as Hamo shrugged and wandered back to the barn.

'Thanks.' Timothy's smile was one of pure relief, but it changed midway when he caught sight of Clara's face.

If she'd been angry before she was furious now, the brief pause enough to reinflate her sails. Pushing his arms away, she faced him angrily.

'I didn't do it to save your skin,' she snapped. 'The fact is I hate violence or perhaps more to the point no doubt I'd have been the one who ended up suturing you and stuck in the obs ward for the next forty-eight hours feeding you through a straw.'

'So we both got lucky.' Timothy grinned, totally unfazed by her anger. 'Can we go back to being friends now?'

'We never were friends,' Clara retorted. 'I'd hardly even class you as a brief acquaintance.'

'Oh, and I suppose you go around kissing all your brief acquaintances like that?'

His humour, if you could call it that, was so appalling Clara could scarcely believe the tiny laugh that escaped her lips, but somewhere in mid-laugh it changed to a sob, and as a tell-tale tear worked its way out Timothy politely pretended not to notice.

'Is there somewhere we can sit down? Preferably on something that isn't made of hay, or I'll be sneezing all night.' She was in no position to answer, tears were choking her now, and when Timothy took her by the hand and led her to a wooden bench she followed him without resistance, sitting on the edge and digging in her bag for a tissue.

'You're supposed to have a silk handkerchief,' Clara sniffed, producing a huge ream of toilet paper.

'I dropped it when I heard Hamo coming.'

They sat in silence for a moment or two, Timothy looking up at the endless stars, one hand loosely over the back of the bench behind her as Clara wept quietly on, blowing her nose and wishing he'd just go away then changing her mind when his hand reached for her shoulder and pulled her in. He let her cry without words, just patting her shoulder and waiting patiently till she'd reached the gulping stage before finally she spoke.

'How did you know I liked him in that way? Is it that obvious?'

'Only to me.' She felt him shrug beneath her cheek. 'I know I'm good-looking and everything, I know women swoon whenever I approach.' He laughed and caught her wrist when she playfully thumped his chest. 'But when you dropped those notes I knew it wasn't because of my devilish charm. I figured Shelly had said something to upset you, and when I heard about Kell and Abby getting engaged, well, it seemed to fit.

'I know you don't believe me, I know you think I'm interfering, but it really would have been a bad move to tell him.'

'Maybe not,' she argued. 'Maybe if he—'

'Clara.' Timothy pulled her face up. Cupping her chin with his hand, he gazed into her tear-filled eyes. 'You look adorable tonight, Kell's had too much to drink and once he finds out that Abby's done a runner he's going to be devastated. It doesn't take Einstein to work out where it would all end up.'

Clara blinked back at him, her forehead furrowing, positive his lips were twitching as he stared back at her.

'Bed,' Timothy said patiently.

'Maybe that's what I wanted,' Clara said defiantly, but Timothy just shook his head, any hint of a laugh fading as he stared back at her.

'No, it isn't, Clara. You think that's what you wanted, but you know deep down that you'd have hated yourself in the morning. And worse, far worse, you'd have lost Kell as a friend.'

'How do you know?' The anger was back in her voice now. Pushing his hand away, she stood up, half expecting him to grab her, to pull her back beside him, but Timothy sat unmoved. 'Maybe bed's exactly where I wanted it to end up. And if you hadn't decided to play the moral majority maybe bed's where I'd be heading right now. And I tell you this much, Timothy, right now it sounds like a far better option than this!'

'Go on, then, go back in there, go and tell him how you're feeling, but half a bottle of wine and a broken heart really doesn't put you in the best position to make rational decisions. Take it from someone who knows.'

She stood for a moment, torn with indecision, knowing Timothy to be right yet praying he was wrong.

'We've all made mistakes,' Timothy ventured, sensing weakness. 'We've all had our hearts stomped on.'

'Please.' Clara flashed a tear-filled glare at him.

'What would a good-looking doctor know about a broken heart?'

'Plenty.' He smiled. 'I've only been a good-looking doctor for a year, remember. Eighteen months ago I fell hook, line and sinker for one of the RNs on a surgical ward, and when I say I was besotted by her I mean I was seriously besotted. I had the ring picked out before I'd even plucked up the courage to ask her on a date. She was seriously stunning. The only trouble was, I was working as a nurse's aide…'

'You were a nurse's aide?'

'I had to pay my bills. Anyway it was good experience, taught me how to actually speak to patients, which is something even the best medical schools don't even touch. Anyway, Rhonda never even glanced in my direction, not even once, until we were at a party. You know the type—a load of doctors, nurses and med students and way too much booze and suddenly she was all over me.' He gave a cheeky grin. 'It was the best night of my life. I'll spare you the details, but I'm sure you get the picture. She was on an early shift and I told her I'd see her later that day at work and we'd go out for dinner, maybe go and see a band or something.'

'Sounds nice,' Clara commented.

'It would have been,' Timothy agreed. 'Only, when she saw me on the ward the next day in my nurse's aide uniform her face dropped a mile and she told me that she couldn't possibly meet me later, that something had come up. And that was that.'

'She dumped you for that?'

Timothy winced and nodded. 'Of course, I should have told her I was really a medical student, that one day she'd get the doctor she so clearly wanted.'

'Why didn't you?'

Timothy shrugged. 'Too much false pride, I guess. I wanted her to want me for me.'

'Fair enough.'

After a moment's thought she sat down beside him.

'The story doesn't end there, though.' His arm slid behind her in what should have comforting brotherly sort of way but suddenly Clara was having terrible trouble breathing. 'There's going to be a huge post-script.'

When Clara didn't respond he carried on regardless. 'After I finish here I'm going to do my diving course and I'm going to walk back onto that surgical ward with a white coat on, tanned as brown as a conker, and...'

'And what?'

'I don't know.' Timothy frowned. 'The fantasy gets a bit hazy there. Either we'll walk off into the sunset and live happily ever after, or I'll be terribly cruel and pretend I don't even remember her name and totally ignore her relentless advances. I haven't quite worked the ending out yet, but when I do I'll let you know.'

'Revenge is a dish best eaten cold,' Clara said with more than a trace of bitterness, smiling when she saw Timothy's startled expression.

'It's an Arabic saying,' she explained. 'I have the same sort of fantasies, I think it's because I watch too many soaps.'

'What's your favourite?'

'My favourite soap or my favourite fantasy?' Clara sighed. 'OK, you asked for it. I dream that maybe one day Kell will wake up and realise how much he adores me, realise that he simply can't live without me, and when he tells me I'll just shrug and say he's too late, that I've moved on, that…' Her voice trailed off, the tears starting again as she realised the futility behind so many wasted dreams.

'What do I do now, Timothy?' The indecision in her voice was so alien that for a moment there even she didn't recognise it. She was a bush nurse, for heaven's sake, used to thinking on her feet, used to making life-and-death decisions completely unaided, but right here, right now she'd never felt more unsure in her life.

'Go home,' Timothy said gently.

'I can't.' Clara shook her head. As appealing as his suggestion was, there were a million and one jobs to be done tonight and most had Clara's name on them. 'There are the chairs to be stacked, the barn to be—'

'You'd have left it for Kell,' Timothy pointed out, 'so why not let someone else do it?' He had her hand now and was leading her away from the barn, away from Kell and a half a life's worth of dreams. And after only a moment's hesitation, after only a tiny glance backwards, Clara realised, to her own amazement, that she was meekly walking away with Timothy taking the lead.

Walking away with barely a backward glance.

CHAPTER THREE

'MORNING!' Ever cheerful, rubbing his hands against the crisp morning air, Timothy breezed into the clinic as Clara concentrated rather too intently on the pile of surgical gloves and suture equipment she was faithfully stocking. 'Where is everyone?'

'They should be along soon,' Clara mumbled, blushing to the roots of her foiled tips, shy and utterly unable to meet his eyes.

'The staff or the patients?'

'Both,' Clara answered weakly. 'Ross has been here since the crack of dawn, admitting a labouring woman who's in room one. He's just raced home to grab some breakfast, he shouldn't be much longer.'

'Do you want me to hold the fort?'

'Sorry?'

'If you need to go in with her, I can watch here.'

Clara shook her head, finally realising where Timothy was coming from. 'She's fine. Her mother's with her. The aboriginal women generally prefer to be left to themselves when they're in labour.'

Surprisingly Timothy nodded. 'It was the same in Adelaide.' He gave a wry laugh. 'Personally I'd be screaming from the rafters and demanding every intervention known to mankind.'

'Me, too.' Still she couldn't meet his eyes, but such was her relief at the near normality of their conversation Clara even managed a small smile. 'Still, it's good that they trust us enough to come to the clinic.

It's important we respect their wishes, so I've made sure she's comfortable and if she needs anything they'll let us know. I'm just stocking up. Go and grab yourself a coffee.'

'Sounds good. Do you want one?'

'I'm fine, thanks.'

Only when he had ducked into the kitchen did she managed to string two breaths together. Yesterday had been spent cringing under her duvet cover, mortified at how close she had come to confronting Kell and reeling in horror at the lengths to which Timothy had had to go to stop her. She'd prayed to be struck down by something horribly contagious so she could hide from the world for a fortnight or so.

All to no avail.

'Did Ross tell Kell?'

He was back, talking in a theatrical whisper and grinning like an eager puppy as he awaited the latest instalment, utterly oblivious to Clara's discomfort.

'I assume so.' Clara shrugged, realigning the boxes of gloves for the umpteenth time. 'I only saw Ross for two minutes this morning, just long enough to get a quick handover, and apart from that I haven't seen anyone since…' Her voice trailed off as her blush deepened. 'Since I left you.'

'Me neither,' Timothy said.

The silence was awful and, putting her bravest foot forward, Clara turned around tentatively. She stared somewhere in the location of his left cheek, completely unable to meet his eyes, grateful that Timothy didn't make a comment about her heavy, swollen, red eyelids.

'Thank you.' When Timothy raised a quizzical eyebrow she elaborated further. 'You were right to stop me from saying anything and I'm only sorry—'

'Forget it.' Timothy broke in, waving his hand dismissively, his easy smile staying firmly in place. 'I'm just relieved we're talking. I've actually been psyching myself to come over for the last hour or so. I was terrified of the reception you'd give me.'

'Me?' Clara asked, startled.

'Yes, you.' Timothy grinned. 'I was half expecting to get a slap on the cheek or something. If I'd known the number of the clinic I'd have been tempted to ring in sick!'

'You didn't look very nervous,' Clara pointed out, grinning in spite of herself.

'I'm a good actor. Look, I probably had no right to interfere, no right to step in the way I did and mess up your plans. I just can't help myself sometimes.'

'Well, I'm glad you did.'

'And I'm glad you're glad, if that makes sense. Shall we start again? Forget everything that's happened and start over.'

Accepting his handshake, Clara gave a small nod and finally managed to look at him, not for long, just for a second or two, but long enough to know that, as good as Timothy's offer sounded, as much as ten minutes ago she'd have given everything she possessed to wipe the slate clean, to obliterate Saturday night's disaster from living memory and banish it from both their minds. Right here, right now, staring into those smiling green eyes, looking up at that open honest face, Clara knew that it simply wasn't going to happen.

Somewhere in mid-handshake, life became terribly complicated all of a sudden.

Somewhere along the way she caught the scent of his aftershave, remembered how it felt to be held by those hands, the weight of his lips on hers, the scorching kiss that she had forcibly pushed from her mind, a moment in time she'd been too embarrassed to re-live…

Until now.

Now the events of Saturday night were rushing back in to her consciousness, playing over and over in her mind with glaring clarity, but her near miss with Kell barely got a look in, and judging by the slightly questioning look in Timothy's eyes, from the subtle increase in his breathing and a nervous tongue running over his lips, Timothy was remembering it, too.

'Friends?' she croaked, forgetting to pull her hand back, barely managing to get the single word out.

'Friends,' Timothy agreed. If anything, his voice was even less steady than Clara's. His warm hand was still on hers, green eyes practically obliterated by his dilating pupils as the world seemed to stop for a moment. Only the untimely appearance of Ross snapped them both to attention, causing a flurry of nervous coughing as their hands shot back and those surgical gloves came under another barrage of scrutiny, this time from both a doctor and a nurse.

'Hi, guys.' Oblivious to the simmering tension, Ross came and parked himself on the nurse's desk as Clara gratefully headed for the kitchen.

'Do you want a coffee, Ross? I was just going to make one.'

'In a bit.' Ross's voice was grim and when Clara actually looked at him she realised Ross wasn't his usual sunny self.

'What's up, Ross?'

'Plenty.' He flashed a wry grin at Timothy. 'Sorry to leave you on your own yesterday but a few things came up.'

'No problem,' Timothy said easily, the silence growing as they waited for Ross to fill it.

'How's Mary doing?'

'Very well.' Clara smiled. 'The contractions are full on now, but Louanna said again that they just wanted to be left alone as much as possible and that she'd call if they wanted anything.'

With business out of the way, Ross had no choice but to break the news.

'Kell's leaving.' For a moment he didn't elaborate, just let the news sink in as Clara stood there, stunned. She could feel Ross's eyes on her, Timothy's, too, and knew they were both expecting some sort of reaction.

'I'm sorry, Clara,' Ross said gently. 'I know this is going to be hard, on you especially.' Startled she looked from Ross to Timothy. Surely he hadn't told him! But her confusion turned to relief as Ross continued. 'I've already put the vacancy on every nursing agency in the phone book, but it might be a while before we get someone.'

'When is he going?' Clara asked, expecting a fortnight, a month even, but nothing prepared her for Ross's answer.

'At the end of the week. But we had a long talk about things yesterday and the upshot is that Kell's finished working at the clinic as of now. He's going to spend the rest of the week packing and sorting out his paperwork.'

'Doesn't he have to serve his notice?' Timothy

asked, his practical questions such a contrast to the emotions that were coursing through Clara.

'He offered to,' Ross sighed. 'The thing is, Timothy, that's not how we run things here. Over the years Kell's put in way above what his contract dictates. Everyone chips in here, and at the end of the day that's how somehow we manage to run a clinic with limited staff and resources that's stuck in the middle of nowhere. It's time to pay Kell back for all he's given to Tennengarrah. He wants to go after Abby and I think we owe it to him to support his decision. He's going to move into a flat and find work before he looks her up, so he's got a lot to sort out before he leaves...' He gave a small shrug. 'People have to want to be here.' Ross stood up and seeing Clara's shocked expression mercifully misinterpreted it. 'Shelly said she'll help out as much as she can. She didn't want to come back to work so soon after having Kate.' He gave a wry laugh. 'Actually, she didn't want to come back to nursing, full stop, but it's not as if there's much choice at the moment. I'm sorry, Clara. I can see you're upset. I really will try and get more help.'

'It's not that.' Clara forced a smile. 'I don't mind the extra work. I'll just miss him, that's all.'

'We all will.' Ross agreed. 'You more than most, no doubt. You've been friends and colleagues for ages.'

Clara nodded, the lump in her throat not really permitting much else, but thankfully Timothy managed to fill the awful gap that followed.

'I don't mind pitching in. I know I'm not a nurse, but when I was a medical student I worked nights as a nurse aide, so I'm more than happy to wear two caps—not literally of course.' He laughed. 'We can't have Clara running herself ragged.'

'Thanks,' Ross said warmly. 'It's just as well you turned up early. How do you fancy being thrown in at the deep end?'

Timothy grinned. 'It's my favourite pastime. Mind you, I normally have an air tank.'

'Timothy dives,' Clara explained, finally managing to resume the conversation, but her heart really wasn't in it.

'Well, Kell was supposed to be doing a mobile clinic this morning…'

'I don't mind,' Clara volunteered, more than happy to be out on the road, but Ross shook his head. 'Kell finally persuaded Jim to have that testicular lump looked at, and it's probably not very politically correct but, given that this is the bush, I think it would be better if a guy went along.'

'I'd need a map,' Timothy said hesitantly, 'and a quick read up on testicular lumps before I head off.'

'We're not that cruel.' Ross laughed. 'I wouldn't send you out on your own on your first day here! You can go to a mobile clinic with Clara later in the week—they take a bit of getting used to so it's best if you just watch the first few times. I'll do the mobile clinic today if you don't mind staying here and running the morning surgery. Normally Monday mornings are pretty much routine, sore throat and ears, a few stitches perhaps. If you don't know how anything works, just ask Clara.'

Oh, she tried, she really tried not to roll her eyes, but as both men turned to her she did exactly that. 'We'll be fine, Ross,' Clara sighed. 'You go on ahead.'

* * *

'How are you doing?'

It was the emptiest the clinic had been all morning. The second Ross had driven off, the floodgates had opened and every ailment that had been put on hold in preparation for the ball had chosen today to surface. Given Timothy's relative inexperience, Clara braced herself for endless questions, but apart from the occasional prompt as to where things were kept Timothy had pretty much rolled his sleeves up and got on with the job. The older locals had been fine, chatting easily to the new doctor, offering to 'shout' him a beer even, but some of the younger guys hadn't been overly friendly with Timothy, taking it upon themselves to act like a collective group of protective older brothers and returning his attempts at small talk with the most suspicious stares and surly remarks. Not that Timothy seemed bothered. He just got right on with the job in hand, happy to ask Clara's opinion every now and then or to advise the patient to come back for a follow-up visit when Ross returned when he felt a more experienced physician's opinion might be called for. To Clara's pleasant surprise, the morning clinic passed smoothly.

'I'll just finish these stitches and then we should be able to grab a coffee.'

'Sounds good to me.' Timothy peered over her shoulder, smiling at the young man who eyed him suspiciously. 'Make sure you take all the antibiotics, Mitch, and come back if there are any problems.' Lowering his voice for Clara's ears only, Timothy moved in over her shoulder. 'I'm sorry if I've been a real pain this morning.'

'You haven't,' Clara conceded, feeling guilty for

her eye-rolling earlier. 'You've done really well. Before you put the kettle on, could you put your head into Mary's room? Tell her I'll be along soon. I just gave her some pethidine before I started this, so hopefully it will be taking effect.'

'Done.' He turned to go then changed his mind. 'Can I watch—I mean when Mary has the baby? If it causes her any embarrassment then, of course, I won't…'

'That'll be fine,' Clara smiled warmly. 'Hopefully it won't be too much longer now.'

'I'll see about that coffee.'

Famous last words!

Settling back to work, Clara snipped the last of the stitches then placed a wad of Melanin and a neat bandage over Mitch's hand, but just as she was sure a well-earned break was finally imminent a commotion brewing outside forced a low sigh to escape from behind her mask.

'Sounds like Hamo's not at his sunniest,' Mitch volunteered, as a few loud expletives winged their way into Theatre. 'Do you need a hand? I can usually calm him down.'

'Better not,' Clara sighed. 'He's usually pretty good for me.' Securing the bandage with tape, she handed Mitch the antibiotics, hating to rush her patient but knowing she was needed elsewhere. 'Make sure you do as Timothy says, and if there's any problems come straight back.'

Jumping off her stool, she discarded all the sharps then followed the noise to the nurse's desk, hoping Hamo wasn't going to take his obvious bad mood out on Timothy. Aggression in the workplace was unfortunately par for the course these days, whatever part of the world you lived in, but as trained as the staff were to deal with it, it was hardly a great first day welcome for Timothy. Hamo occasionally turned up at the clinic the worst for wear, needing stitches or whatever, but one look at him and Clara knew that in this instance more was going to be called for. His face was tinged grey and he was clutching his stomach with one fist, the other dividing its time between holding onto the desk at the nurses' station and punching in the air as he cursed the world at large and Timothy in particular.

'Hamo, what's wrong?' Clara asked, making sure she didn't get too close.

'I need some painkillers and the so-called doctor here won't give them to me.'

'I didn't say that, Hamo.' Timothy's voice was calm, laid back even, much to Clara's relief. With Hamo in this volatile mood even the slightest hint of confrontation could turn things ugly, but Timothy seemed to know exactly what he was doing. His stance, though confident, was non-confrontational and Clara listened as he carried on talking, all the time watching Hamo. 'I can see that you're in a great deal of pain, but before I can give you anything I need to examine you.'

'I just need an injection,' Hamo snarled through gritted teeth, staggering towards them, and Clara realised with a surge of nervousness that his short fuse had really snapped this time. But Timothy had obviously read the situation the same way and in one swift motion he pulled Clara out of the way and moved himself forward, effectively standing between her and the patient.

'Why don't you go and check on Mary?' Timothy

suggested, as Hamo doubled over again. And though Timothy's voice was calm, friendly even, Clara knew it was an order and not a request, though she had no intention of following it. Hamo was a tricky customer at the best of times but Clara had always been positive he would never lift a finger to her.

She wasn't so sure that courtesy would be extended to Timothy.

'I'd rather stay here,' Clara said firmly, but Timothy shook his head.

'We'll be fine, won't we, Hamo?' For the first time he looked at Clara. 'Once I've explained to him that we've a young woman here about to give birth, he'll settle down. He's hardly going to knock out the only doctor for miles and put a woman and her baby's life at risk.' Turning back to the patient, he gave him a smile. 'Right, let's have a look at you, then,' he said. Deliberately ignoring Hamo's reluctance and taking his elbow, he guided him to the trolley. 'That's the man,' Timothy said matter-of-factly. 'Up on the trolley so I can have a look at you and then we'll see about pain control.'

Suitably impressed, Clara undressed Hamo and tried to take a set of obs as Timothy slipped an oxygen mask over his face and attempted to get a history. 'What's been happening, Hamo?'

'I just want an injection.'

'Not until I know what's wrong with you. How about you tell me when this pain started?'

'How about you give me a needle?' Hamo was getting agitated again and Clara took over.

'Hamo, enough. Let the doctor have a look at you and answer his questions. And I need you to stay still so that I can run a set of obs on you.'

But Hamo was having none of it. Pulling off his mask, he tried to lever himself off the trolley, which wasn't a good move as the brakes weren't on and the trolley lurched forward, unfortunately clipping Clara none too gently on the hip.

'Hamo.' Pushing on the brakes with his foot, Timothy's voice for the first time wasn't quite so laid back. 'Lie down. You're not going anywhere because you're not well enough. Now the quicker you answer my questions the quicker I can make a diagnosis, but I *cannot* give you an injection until I'm sure what's going on.' His eyes met Clara's but the annoyance in his voice didn't abate. 'Now, Clara, can you, please, check on Mary?'

'Can I have a quick word, Timothy?' Widening her eyes for Timothy's benefit, Clara kept her voice even. 'About Mary.'

He gave a brief nod then turned his attention back to his patient.

'I'm not going to fight you, Hamo. If you want my help you can have it, but that has to be your call. Now, lie there for a moment and decide whether or not you're prepared to co-operate. I'll be back shortly.'

Only when they were out of earshot did they speak.

'I assume this isn't about Mary?'

Clara nodded. 'I know Hamo's being obnoxious, but the truth is, Timothy, in all the time I've known him he's never been aggressive towards me. I just wanted you to be clear on that. And he's never once asked for an injection—it normally takes a supreme effort to get him to take even the mildest painkiller. It isn't drugs that he's after, I'm sure of that. He must be in a lot of pain to be acting this way.'

'I don't doubt that he is,' Timothy said thought-fully. 'Thanks, Clara, I'll take it on board. I'm actu-ally seriously concerned about him. I'll have to ex-amine him, of course, but I'm pretty sure he's going to need more care than we can offer here.'

'Do you want me to get the Flying Doctors on the line?' Clara offered.

'I'll just have a look first—hopefully he's calmed down a bit by now. Oh, and, Clara.' Turning, she paused, expecting a quick question, but from the look on Timothy's face she realised he wasn't best pleased. 'Next time there's a violent situation and I ask you to leave, please, don't argue the point.'

'I wasn't arguing.' Clara flushed. 'Like I said, I've known Hamo all my life. I'm sure he'd never hurt me.'

'Sure's not good enough,' Timothy said grimly. 'Suppose he'd lashed out in pain or tried to hit me and missed, suppose he'd ended up blacking your eye.'

'I'd have been all right,' Clara answered quickly, but from the look on his face it was clearly the wrong answer.

'Maybe you would have been, but how do you think Hamo would have felt afterwards and how would the rest of the town have dealt with him when word got out? You come with a lot of surrogate broth-ers, Clara, I saw that for myself on Saturday night. And while I'm not excusing violence, sometimes the lines get blurred when a patient's in pain. Sometimes we have to save them from themselves.'

She'd never thought of it like that and, suitably chastised, Clara turned away. 'I'll just check on Mary,' she murmured, but only as she walked off did she realise the full horror of the situation Timothy had just averted and her hands were shaking slightly as she knocked on the door of the side room and walked in.

'How are things?'

'Better.' Louanna looked up from her daughter. 'What was all the noise about outside?'

'One of the patients got a bit upset,' Clara said tactfully, 'but it's all sorted now. I'm sorry if it upset Mary.'

'She didn't hear a thing,' Louanna said softly. 'That injection really helped. She's even managed to doze off. Things seem to be slowing down—the labour won't just stop, will it?'

'I'll just have a little look. I'll try and not disturb her,' Clara said, moving quietly and checking the baby's heart rate with the foetal monitor then standing with her hand on Mary's stomach for a few moments. 'The baby's heart rate is good and strong. I'm not going to wake her and do an internal. I'm sure things are moving on just as they should.'

'So why have the pains stopped?'

'That's mother nature giving Mary a chance to catch her breath before the real hard work of pushing starts,' Clara said assuredly. 'Just let her rest and when she wakes, or if you need anything at all, just come and let me know.'

Timothy had been busy while she had been away. IV fluids had been run through a line and were hung beside the gurney on a pole as he inserted an IV bung. Hamo was still in obvious pain, but the aggression of previously seemed to have subsided. He was even keeping on his oxygen mask.

'How is she?' Timothy asked, without looking up,

taking a large syringe of blood from the IV bung as Clara hovered with the IV line.

'Resting. How's Hamo?'

'Still in pain, but more compliant now. He let me take a set of obs.' The worried grimace Timothy pulled was for Clara's eyes only and he nodded appreciatively as he pulled out the syringe and Clara immediately connected the IV fluids, securing the access with tape while Timothy filled various vials with the blood he had collected. 'Give him a two-hundred-millilitre bolus of fluid, then run the flask over four hours,' Timothy instructed Clara, then turned to Hamo. 'I'm just going to have a word with Clara, Hamo, and then I'll be back with that injection.'

'What do you think is going on?' Clara asked, once they were out of earshot.

'He's got an acute abdomen,' Timothy replied. 'He's in a lot of pain and he's been vomiting since the early hours of the morning.'

'Any blood in it?' Clara asked, but Timothy shook his head.

'None. I've asked him about his alcohol intake…'

'I bet that went down well.' Clara grimaced.

'Actually, when I explained to him why I need to know, he was quite open. He drinks regularly, but even Hamo admits that he excelled himself at the ball on Saturday night. I think he's got acute pancreatitis, and if that's the case he's going to need to be transferred.'

Clara nodded. Pancreatitis was sometimes caused by excessive alcohol consumption and although the treatment was fairly conservative—careful monitoring of IV fluid intake and urine output, along with strict pain control—there were many possible complications, some of which could be life-threatening.

'We haven't got the facilities to do the blood tests for pancreatitis here, but they can be sent of with him when the Flying Doctors come,' Clara said, gesturing to the tubes in the kidney dish Timothy was holding. 'But we've got the urinary test strips that'll do the job. I'll see if he can give us a specimen.'

'I've already asked,' Timothy said grimly. 'And he flatly refused.'

'Well, if it is pancreatitis, he's going to need a catheter. We could get a specimen that way.'

But Timothy shook his head. 'Again, he refuses. Until I give him some pain control I don't think we're going to get much further with him.' He glanced at his watch. 'How much longer do you think Ross will be?'

'An hour, maybe two. Do you want me to try and contact him? Mind you, if he's running the clinic he mightn't hear the radio, and there's no satellite coverage where Ross is so I can't even get him on his mobile.'

Timothy shook his head. 'I might as well talk to the Flying Doctors. It's obvious he needs to be transferred and the quicker we get things moving the better. If you can get the Flying Doctors on the line for me that would be great.'

'What about pain control?' Clara asked, knowing her question wasn't an easy one to answer. Acute abdomens were notoriously difficult to diagnose, and woe betide any junior doctor who gave analgesia without a concrete diagnosis. Once the symptoms were masked by analgesia it would make the surgeon's job of an accurate diagnosis that much harder and could, in fact, prove life-threatening.

'I'll talk to the Flying Doctors first, but the truth is I can't leave him in pain till they arrive.' For a second or two he chewed on his bottom lip then he gave a brief shake of his head, his slightly hesitant stance changing. 'No, I'm confident of my diagnosis. He's got upper abdominal pain after a large drinking episode, he's tachycardic with low blood pressure and his temperature's up, frequent vomiting and he's got a positive Cullen's sign.'

Clara had kept up with Timothy's findings until then, but her slight frown didn't go unnoticed.

'Discoloration around the umbilicus,' Timothy explained. 'This great surgeon in Adelaide pointed it out to me once, and Hamo has got the same thing. Still, I'd feel a lot happier giving him an injection with a positive urine test to back me up. You get the Flying Doctors on the line for me, and while you're taking care of that I'll have another go at persuading Hamo to provide a specimen.'

All to no avail, though.

Timothy had to relay his findings to the very experienced Dr Hall Jells, or Dr Hall as the locals all knew him, and Clara cringed for Timothy, knowing Hall's questions would be brutal. Leaving him for a second, she made a last-ditch attempt to persuade Hamo, but it was a waste of time and she shook her head as she returned, while Timothy rolled his eyes and carried on talking into the telephone.

'I'm fairly confident of my diagnosis.' She watched as he grimaced and held the receiver back an inch from his ear. 'I'm actually very confident,' he said more forcefully, 'and once I've given him an injection

I'm sure he'll be far more compliant.' Replacing the receiver, Timothy gave her a tight smile. 'He said to give him 10 mg of morphine.'

'Hall's a great doctor,' Clara soothed. 'If he didn't think you sounded confident, he'd have told you to hold off.'

'Let's just hope I'm right.'

The morphine had the desired effect, Hamo settled markedly, but his observations remained erratic. His heart beating alarmingly fast and his blood pressure dropped more than could be put down to the effects of the morphine.

'Dr Hall wants a catheter in,' Clara said firmly. 'I know you're embarrassed, Hamo, but it really is necessary.'

A weary nod was the only response she got and Clara gave Timothy a worried look as alarms started going off. 'Lay him flat and give him another two-hundred-millilitre bolus and open up the IV full bore,' Timothy said quickly as he set to work inserting the catheter. 'And turn his oxygen up to ten litres.' Clara did as Timothy ordered, expecting Hamo to protest to being laid down, for the pain in his abdomen to make this movement uncomfortable, but as Hamo meekly lay back on the gurney Clara's panic mode upped a notch.

'I think I preferred him angry,' Timothy muttered. 'Right, I've got a specimen.' He handed the small jar to Clara who tested it as Timothy inserted a second IV line into Hamo's other arm to enable them to give him more fluids. 'We have to watch that we don't overload him, though. With pancreatitis they can tip into pulmonary oedema quickly. What does his urine test show?'

'It's positive,' Clara said, holding the dipstick up to the colour chart on the bottle and holding it up for Timothy to see. 'Your diagnosis was spot on.'

There was no sigh of relief, no smug smile on Timothy's face as his difficult diagnosis was confirmed, just a worried frown as he worked on his patient. 'At least we know what we're dealing with. What's his blood pressure doing now?'

'It's coming up,' Clara responded. 'Ninety on forty. Could this be from the morphine?'

Timothy shook his head, flashing a light into Hamo's eyes as he did so. 'I don't think so. His pupils are still dilated and his breathing rate's high. It's the pancreatitis that's causing his collapse. Young men often compensate for a while then drop their blood pressure suddenly, but it's coming up now,' he added with quiet satisfaction.

Hamo started to move around, pulling again at the mask. He was still deathly pale but at least there was a bit of fight back in him now, but even before he started to retch, many years of nursing told Clara what was coming next and she deftly raised the head of the trolley while simultaneously reaching for a kidney dish.

'Do you want an NG tube in?' Clara asked. A nasogastric tube was a soft rubber tube that was passed through the patient's nose and into their stomach. Though the procedure was uncomfortable at the time, once in the tube enabled the stomach contents to be emptied and generally the patient felt a lot more settled.

'Can you do it?' Timothy asked. 'I've only put a couple in before and if he carries on picking up I don't think he'll let me have more than one go and I don't want to cause him more discomfort than necessary.'

'Sure,' Clara agreed, blinking in surprise at Timothy's openness and his overriding concern for the patient's comfort. Most doctors would have battled on, refusing to admit they couldn't do it, more than happy to have a go in the name of experience. But instead Timothy was putting not only the patient's welfare but his comfort first.

It was as refreshing as it was welcome.

Now that Hamo's observations were more stable, now that the crisis had been swiftly and skilfully diverted, the tension in the room subsided a notch. But only a notch. Hamo was still gravely ill and any variance could see him sinking back rapidly into a critical condition.

'Hamo,' Clara said gently, 'I'm going to pass a small tube through your nose and into your stomach. Once it's in you'll feel a lot more comfortable, but it's not very pleasant while I pass it, you might start retching or gagging, but it's very important that you don't pull it out.'

Hamo nodded but as Clara started to insert the tube his good intentions evaporated as his hand instinctively reached to pull it back up. But Timothy was too quick for him, grabbing his arms and clamping them down firmly. Unfortunately, Hamo jerked his head back and the tube came up, which meant Clara would have to start again.

'Come on, Hamo, don't fight me,' Clara said firmly. 'You really need this tube.'

'Sister?' Louanna was at the door, her face concerned. 'I think Mary needs to be seen. She says that she wants to push.'

'You go,' Clara said to Timothy, her mind working ten to the dozen. Second-stage labour in a first baby normally took a while and they really needed to get this tube down. 'Do a set of obs on Mary and the baby. I'll get this tube in and then we'll swap over.' Her eyes locked on Hamo. 'Mary's having her baby, so you need to stay still for me, Hamo. Timothy has to go.'

'Go,' Hamo agreed bravely, gripping the sides of the trolley with his hands and taking a deep breath as Timothy sped off.

Hamo tried, he really did, but as the tube reached the back of his throat again his hands shot up. Thankfully, help was at hand. As he entered the clinic Ross instantly read the situation and sped over to the trolley, gripping Hamo's hands tightly without a word as Clara finished the uncomfortable procedure. Only when the tube was firmly strapped in place did she address her boss.

'Thanks for that.'

'What's been going on?'

They moved out of earshot and Clara gave Ross a brief rundown.

'Hamo came in at the end of clinic with severe abdo pain. He was pretty aggressive, but thankfully he settled with some morphine. The Flying Doctors have been mobilised.'

'What's the diagnosis?'

'Pancreatitis.'

'And that's been confirmed?'

Clara nodded. 'Eventually.' When Ross frowned Clara elaborated, noting his grim face as she explained how Timothy had called in the Flying Doctors and given morphine without the benefit of Hamo's urine test. 'He was great,' she concluded. 'I mean that, Ross. Hamo dropped his blood pressure just before you arrived and it was touch and go for a moment or two, so the last thing he needs is a lecture. I think a pat on the back might be more appropriate.'

'So, do you think we should keep him?' Ross grinned, making his way back to Hamo's bedside. 'Where is he, by the way?'

'Oh, lord,' Clara groaned, casting an anxious eye towards Mary's room. 'I told him I'd be straight in.'

'I'll watch Hamo.' Ross smiled. 'You'd better go where you're most needed.'

She wasn't needed.

In fact, not a single head turned Clara's way as she gently pushed open the door.

Not Mary's, her eyes closed in deep concentration as she bore down, pushing her newborn into the darkened, hushed room.

Not Louanna's, who held her daughter's shoulders, supporting her and staring on in wonder at the unfolding miracle.

And not Timothy's.

The deliciously awkward, eager-to-please young man had vanished. In his place was now a calm and extremely competent doctor, his sleeves rolled up, two large gloved hands holding the infant's head as its shoulders rotated, murmuring words of encouragement in low, confident tones that epitomised the calm feeling in the room.

It was truly a privilege to be there and Clara closed the door quietly, moving in closer—not to interfere, just to observe the beauty of a miracle that never ceased to amaze her, marvelling not only at the wonder of nature but at Timothy's quiet compassion, the love and empathy that seemed to fill the room, giving what could have been just another routine birth the status it deserved.

Even the baby, as it slipped into the world, as Timothy delivered him safely into his mother's outstretched arms, barely let out a cry of protest. Moving quietly closer, Clara watched the unfolding scene, the big dark eyes of the infant blinking at the world around him, his little mouth turning to his mother's breast as she held him ever closer, oblivious to the blankets Clara tucked around them as Timothy worked on, delivering the placenta, quietly unobtrusive but comfortingly there.

'He's all right?'

They were the first words that had been spoken, the almost reverent silence broken by Mary as she dragged her eyes from her newborn and sought Timothy's reassuring ones.

'He's perfect.' Pulling the swaddle of blankets away, Timothy did a very rudimentary check of the newborn. 'I'll check him over properly later, but for now everything's just fine.'

'He hardly cried.'

'He had a gentle welcome,' Clara said softly, just as the baby lost the nipple he was feeding on and the loud wail of protest he made had them all smiling. 'We'll leave you to it now. I'll bring you in a light snack in a just a bit.'

'Thank you,' Mary murmured, turning her eyes back to her newborn as they turned to leave the room. 'Doctor?'

As Timothy turned, she said it again, only this time it was loaded with gratitude, and meaning.

'Thank you.'

* * *

The Flying Doctors always cut a dash.

And as laid back as Clara was at work, she never failed to be impressed when they arrived. She watched out of the window as the white plane touched down, trailing a red haze of dust behind it as it sped along the clinic's runway. The crew made its way speedily over to the clinic, smart in their white and navy uniforms, but however much the scene moved her she knew it didn't come close to what Timothy was feeling, witnessing it for the first time.

The Flying Doctors were an enigma. You didn't have to be Australian to know about the team of men and women who faced the harsh Australian elements daily, the white plane that swooped out of the sky and bought medical technology, knowledge and hope to the most remote of communities, but seeing it for the first time, witnessing a legend close up, was over-whelming to say the least, and Clara smiled to herself as Timothy nervously ran through his handover to Hall, justified his diagnosis and outlined his course of treatment, his Adam's apple bobbing up and down as Hall skimmed through the notes.

'You did a good job, mate.'

It was all Timothy was going to get, but from Hall it was strong praise indeed and Clara caught his eye as Timothy gave a small satisfied nod, a smile on the edge of his lips as he stepped back and let the team take over.

'Look after yourself, Hamo.' Clara smiled as every-one fluttered around, changing over monitors, setting up equipment, moving in the stretcher. Now that his blood pressure had stabilised and the painkillers had kicked in, Hamo was back to his rather gruff self, but the aggression of earlier had gone, leaving him rather shamefaced and subdued.

'I can take care of myself.' He gave a small shrug. 'I'm sorry about before.'

'Let's just forget it, shall we?' Clara said gently. 'You were in pain…'

'It's no excuse.'

'No, it isn't, Hamo,' Clara said thoughtfully, 'but maybe a couple of weeks in hospital will give you some time to think about things.'

'My drinking?'

Clara nodded but didn't say anything. Hamo knew the score—the next move had to be up to him.

'I need to cut down.' When Clara still didn't respond Hamo lay back on the pillow. 'I need to stop, don't I?'

'I think you already know the answer.'

He gave a thin smile then looked up. 'Hey, it's not just me you need to worry about, Clara. I can take care of myself. I'm not so sure that you can, though.'

'What are you talking about, Hamo?' Clara frowned.

'You and the new guy. I saw what happened on Saturday, remember? Just watch yourself. He'll be gone in a few weeks like all the other doctors that drift in and out of Tennengarrah. Look at that Abby Hampton, she didn't even do the full three months.'

'Hamo,' Clara said patiently, 'I'm well aware Timothy's only here for a while, and what you saw on Saturday night…well, it wasn't exactly how it looked. That's all you need to know,' she added quickly, as Hamo started to protest. 'Now, I know you all mean well, I know you guys all think it's your duty to protect me, but I'm pushing thirty now, I'm more than able to look after myself, so if you and your friends can stop giving Timothy the evil eye, it would be much appreciated.'

Hamo gave a reluctant shrug. 'What sort of a name's Timothy anyway? What's wrong with Tim or—'

'Timo?' Clara grinned as Hall made his way back over, ready to move. Hamo finally joined her in a smile. 'You just concentrate on looking after yourself, Hamo. I'll be fine.'

'That birth was beautiful.' They were in the kitchen now, Clara pouring water into two massive mugs as Timothy set to work on the biscuit barrel.

'It was great,' Timothy agreed. 'Look, I hope I haven't put you offside, not coming to get you. It's just when I put my head in she was practically having it, there really wasn't—'

'Timothy,' Clara interrupted, 'Let's stop apologising to each other, shall we? You're a doctor, for heaven's sake, you don't need my permission to deliver a baby.'

'I am, aren't I?' Timothy winked. 'Heavens, I wish I felt more like one.'

'But you've been great this morning,' Clara enthused. 'Hall's not exactly gushing, but he was pretty pleased with your work and I know for a fact Ross was impressed. And as for the delivery...' Clara gestured in the vague direction of Mary's room. 'You were great in there. You couldn't have been better!

'You've no idea how many doctors, I've seen, nurses too come to that, rushing in, lights blazing, taking over, when all most women want is to do it for themselves. You've made this morning very special for Mary.'

'I think the baby took care of that,' Timothy said modestly, but Clara shook her head.

'Mary wasn't even sure she wanted to come to the clinic to have her baby. Now she's going to go back to her people and tell them how well it went, which can only be a good thing. Word of mouth can be our greatest asset but it can have its downsides, too. Hopefully Mary might persuade some of the other women to give the clinic a go now and that can only benefit us all. Have you done many deliveries?'

'Three, though I've seen loads more. I was always begging to be let in, I love the labour room.'

'Me, too.'

'Still,' Timothy admitted, 'it helped that you were only a call away. I don't think I'd have felt quite so confident if I'd been there on my own. That baby really did come quickly at the end—I wasn't trying to play the hero or anything.'

Arranging a tray for Mary, Clara stopped in midmotion, a teacup in mid-air as a smile ghosted across her lips.

'I don't think you have to try, Timothy.' Her back was to him so her voice so soft he probably didn't even hear it. 'I've a feeling playing the hero just comes naturally to you.'

CHAPTER FOUR

NORMALLY Clara loved the mobile clinic.

Loved being out on the road, alone with her thoughts and the treat of a picnic lunch before heading back, driving the Jeep along the endless red roads, assured of a warm welcome from the patients she had nursed over the years.

But not this morning.

This morning, she had been relegated to passenger. Timothy, keen to get his bearings, bumped the clinic's Jeep along, grinding gears and attempting small talk as Clara responded in monosyllables.

But her aloofness had nothing to do with the fact that yet again she was playing nursemaid to a new doctor, or the fact that the prospect of four hours alone with Timothy had her stomach twisting into strange excited knots…

Instead, it had everything to do with the house call they were making *en route*.

Pulling out her next patient's notes, she attempted to read them impassively but failed miserably. Her eyes blurred as she read the hospital doctor's covering letter.

Some days she hated her job.

Looking up from the notes, Clara realised that they'd missed their turning about two minutes ago. 'You were supposed to turn left back there,' she mumbled, fishing in her pocket for a tissue and blowing her nose loudly.

'When?' Slamming on the brakes, Timothy craned his neck as he shot the Jeep into reverse. 'You didn't say.'

'I did,' Clara said through gritted teeth, massaging her neck which had been positively whiplashed as the vehicle had growled in protest. 'I told you to take the next left.'

'Half an hour ago,' Timothy pointed out, clearly as irritated as Clara. 'A reminder wouldn't have gone amiss.'

'You were the one who wanted to get a feel for the area,' Clara snarled. 'Do I look like a talking map?'

They bumped backwards in angry silence, finally locating the turning which, Clara realised, unless you knew it existed, didn't exactly stand out.

Well, she wasn't going to apologise!

'Do you want a quick look at the notes?' Clara offered instead, but Timothy shook his head.

'I had a read before we came and Ross bought me up to scratch. This is the lady with breast cancer and cerebral metastases who doesn't want any further treatment, right? She's having trouble sleeping and I'm to—'

'No!' The force behind her voice came as a surprise to them both and Clara took a couple of deep breaths before she carried on talking. 'This is Eileen Benton, happily married, mother of two wonderful children, who dabbles in ceramics and also happens to have breast cancer.'

'Hey, Clara!' Slamming on the brakes again, Timothy pulled the handbrake on and turned to face her. 'What's your problem this morning?'

'I don't have a problem,' Clara retorted. 'I'm just pointing out that Eileen isn't merely another diagnosis. She also happens to be a beautiful young woman—'

'I'm sure she is,' Timothy broke in, 'and no doubt I'll find that out for myself in a few minutes. Is that what this is about? Do you not think that I'm qualified enough to be treating your precious patients?'

'What are you talking about?'

'Here.' Pulling out his prescription pad, he scribbled furiously on it. 'Temazepam 10 mg—that's what she needs isn't it? Ross said she was having trouble sleeping. As you clearly think I've little to contribute, why don't you go on ahead and see her? And I'll wait in the car.'

'Timothy?' Swallowing hard, Clara realised she'd gone too far, that she'd taken her rather pensive mood out on him when it simply wasn't his fault and an explanation was called for. 'It's not you I'm upset with.'

'Isn't it? You've made it blatantly clear you don't want me along this morning. I've been trying to talk to you the whole way here and you've completely ignored me, which is fine. If that's how you want to work then that's your right, but when it comes to the patients' care don't take your bad mood out on me. I was merely attempting to check I'd got a handle on her diagnosis before I walk in there. Now, if I'm not quite up on all the patients marital statuses and pastimes it has nothing to do with me being an unfeeling bastard and everything to do with the fact I've been in this town less than a week.'

'She's a friend.' The catch in her voice took the wind out his sails for a moment. She heard his sharp intake of breath, saw his knuckles loosen their grip slightly on the steering-wheel. 'I know practically everyone in this town, but Eileen really is a good friend. I was a bridesmaid at her wedding, I delivered her babies…' Swallowing hard, Clara fought back her tears—the last thing she wanted was for Eileen to see her with red glassy eyes. 'That's why I've been quiet in the car.' She gave a small shrug. 'Rude even. I just really don't want to do this.'

'Did you tell Ross?' he asked gently. 'Maybe Shelly should be the one to look after her.'

'I asked Ross if he'd mind sending Shelly, but apparently she got upset when she heard that Eileen was refusing any further treatment…'

'So did you,' Timothy pointed out, but Clara just gave a wry laugh.

'Ah, but I don't have children that are around the same age. Apparently it makes it worse.' Leaning over, she checked her reflection in the rear-view mirror, then blew her nose again. 'I'm probably being a bit unfair. I'm sure if I'd reminded Ross just how close Eileen and I are he wouldn't have sent me. I should have stood up for myself a bit more.'

'Do you want me to go in,' Timothy offered, 'by myself? I could walk to the house from here and say that I got a bit lost. She won't even know you're here.'

Clara shook her head. 'I'm fine now.' Jumping out, she pulled out her bag and waited as Timothy got out, a shy smile on her lips as he walked over. 'And I'm sorry about earlier. I'm actually really glad you're here.'

'Clara! I'm so glad it's you.'

Stepping inside, Clara's misgivings were instantly dispelled. The warmth of Eileen's welcome, the obvious delight that she was there, told Clara there and then that the pain of nursing Eileen would be worth it. Nursing mightn't be the most glamorous job in the world but the relationships forged with patients were always special and none more so when they were friends.

Agony though this journey they were embarking on would undoubtedly be, Clara vowed at that moment that they would travel it together with dignity and affection, strengthening their friendship as they faced the unknown together.

'Happy birthday!'

'Eileen!' Clara let out a small moan of embarrassed protest as a brightly coloured package was thrust at her. 'You shouldn't have.'

'Why on earth not? It's your birthday after all. So, what else did you get—anything nice?'

Clara gave a small shrug. 'Nothing yet,' she mumbled, quickly changing the subject. 'Eileen, this is Timothy Morgan, he's the new doctor in Tennengarrah,'

She waited as they shook hands but Eileen hadn't finished embarrassing her yet. 'Are you trying to tell me that no one even remembered your birthday? What about Bill, Ross and Shelly, Kell—'

'I hate a fuss, you know that,' Clara broke in. 'Ross and Shelly will do something tonight, no doubt, at Kell's leaving do, he's got his head in the clouds— I'll fill you in on all that later. And Bill's hardly in a position to go shopping. Did you hear he had the operation in the end? He's doing very well apparently.'

'Is that a lecture I can feel coming on?' Eileen's smile never faltered, but there was a notable tension in the room as Clara fumbled with the wrapping paper. 'I know you, Clara, and I also know where you're leading. Bill changed his mind and just look how well it's all worked out.'

'I'm not here to lecture you, Eileen,' Clara said softly, staring at the small bowl covered in bright ceramic pieces, a glorious picture of the sun and the moon and hundreds of tiny silver stars. It would have taken for ever to make and, given Eileen's fragile health, it made it all the more special. 'This is beautiful, I'll treasure it.'

She'd sworn to herself that she wouldn't cry, sworn that she'd get through this without even a hint of a tear, but looking up at her friend Clara realised she wasn't alone with her tears as Eileen sobbed quietly. She wished she could go over there, put her arms around her friend and tell her she thought she was doing the right thing, but she couldn't.

Couldn't watch Eileen give up on her life with hardly a fight.

'You've been having trouble sleeping since the metastases were diagnosed?'

It was Timothy who spoke, his voice so strong and clear that for a moment it sounded as if it didn't belong and Clara felt a stirring of anger for his apparent callousness, which she quickly fought to check, reminding herself that it was the diagnosis that was callous, not Timothy.

'I slept well at the hospital,' Eileen gulped. 'In fact, that's just about all that I did! It's just since I've come home that I've been having trouble. I get all worked out about silly things. I'm fine during the day, I just get on with things…'

'No doubt you're busy.' Timothy gestured to the pile of toys in the corner. 'How old are your children?'

'Seven and four. Rhiannon's at school, Heidi's having a nap at the moment—you'll see her soon, no doubt. Like I said, during the day I'm fine...' Her voice trailed off and Clara ached to fill it, didn't want Timothy to push yet she knew he had to.

'But at night?' Timothy said gently as Eileen buried her face in her hands, the weight of the horrible cloud that hung over her too heavy for her thin tired shoulders.

'I make lists.' Eileen's voice was a strangled whisper. Pulling a piece of paper from the coffee-table, she held it in the air and a strangled sob followed. Clara felt like joining in, but she sat quietly as Timothy made his way over, joining Eileen on the settee, not remotely awkward, not uncomfortable, just tender and gentle and infinitely patient as he took the paper and read it quietly.

'Rhiannon loves cucumber in her sandwiches, but she doesn't like the skin,' Eileen said softly as Timothy carried on reading. 'And Heidi can only sleep if she has her favourite blanket. Jerry knows that, of course, but she doesn't just like it over her, she likes the top part tucked under her cheek, and even though she says she doesn't want apple juice in the morning, she wants it really.' Her voice was shaking, her hands too as she took the list back from Timothy. 'It probably seems stupid. I know they're all going to be fine, that they'll be well looked after. I know I can't put everything down on paper, can't sum up their little personalities in a few pages. It's just...' Her voice trembled. 'It's just that...'

'Maybe you're not ready to hand them over yet?' Timothy suggested softly, as Clara held her breath, watching in awe as Timothy gently pushed further.

'Are you having second thoughts about cancelling the treatment?'

'I don't know.' Eileen's voice was almost angry. 'I just don't know if I can go through it all again, and more to the point I don't know if I can put Jerry and the kids through it again. The last lot of chemo was hell on earth, but at the time I figured it was worth it. That I'd beat the cancer and get on with the rest of my life. Now I'm being told I need radiation treatment, possibly surgery and if I'm very lucky I might even get a follow-up round of chemo to top the whole lot off. And for what? A few more months?'

'It might be a lot more than that,' Timothy said, but seeing Eileen shake her head he looked at her thoughtfully for a moment before changing tack. 'Suppose you're right, suppose that the worst-case scenario comes to fruition and all you get out of this is a few more months, what would that give you?'

Eileen looked up at him puzzled.

'Where will six months see your family?'

'Heidi would be at school,' Eileen whispered.

'I don't have children,' Timothy volunteered, 'but, from what I've heard, that makes a big difference. Once they're off at school during the day things get a bit easier, don't they?'

Eileen nodded. 'If the worst does happen, even though Jerry says he'll manage, I know that at least if both the girls were at school it would make things easier for him.'

'For the girls, too, perhaps,' Timothy suggested. 'Routine can be very comforting. What else?'

Eileen gave a small teary smile. 'Rhiannon's eighth birthday, our tenth wedding anniversary.'

'Worth fighting for?'

Eileen nodded, but her face was lined with indecision. 'Is it fair on them, though? I'd have to go to
Adelaide for all the treatment—a half-hour appointment is a three-day round trip.'

Clara saw Timothy frown and broke in. 'The air
ambulance only takes patients while they're unwell.
When Eileen has her radiation treatment she'll qual-
ify, but if it's just a follow-up visit or a regular con-
sultation she has to take the bus. That's a day there
and a day back for a half-hour appointment.'

Eileen nodded. 'And if it doesn't work, that's time
I could have spent with them.'

Retrieving the list, Timothy read it again closely,
not answering her question at first. 'You're wrong,
Eileen, there's nothing stupid about this list, I happen
to think it's beautiful. This is the type of thing the
children will treasure one day. One look at this and
they'll know how much you love them, and hopefully
you'll be around to read it with them. They need you,
Eileen, and you need them.' His voice changed.
Snapping back into doctor mode, he handed her over
the bottle of pills. 'One at bedtime. Only take one,
mind, because if you wake up in the night and can't
get back to sleep you can take another one. They're
pretty short-acting and won't leave you feeling
groggy the next day, but I've a feeling you won't be
needing them once you make up your mind. Do you
want me to get Ross to speak to the specialists in
Adelaide?'

When Eileen didn't answer straight away, he carried on talking. 'Just because you start treatment, it
doesn't mean you can't change your mind later.
You're still in control here and Clara and I will sup-

port you in whatever you decide.' Looking over, he smiled as Clara stepped forward.

'Why don't you talk it over with Jerry? I'll call back tomorrow,' Clara suggested gently, holding back the sigh of relief as Eileen finally nodded.

They didn't talk about it in the Jeep. He seemed to sense she was just too raw to go over things, but far from the strained journey earlier this time, when Timothy made small talk, Clara responded warmly, even managing a laugh or two at his appalling jokes. And later, as they ran the mobile clinic, as she watched him interact with the locals. Not once did she need to interrupt, not once did she take him to one side and warn him the way things were done out here.

A strange well of pride, a flutter of excitement grew in her stomach as she watched him work. A junior doctor he might be, but Clara knew that it was only a matter of time before he found his feet and the world would be all the richer for having him. Timothy was a true doctor in every sense of the word. He had it all—tenderness, compassion, wisdom and all topped with that generous smile, and Clara wondered how she could ever have thought him awkward.

Timothy Morgan was going to be one helluva doctor.

They lay on the rug, laughing immoderately at Timothy's silly jokes, and Clara didn't mind for a moment having the new guy along with her, didn't mind sharing her picnic lunch or the quiet time she normally adored.

In fact, she relished it.

'That would have to be the best picnic I've ever tasted,' Timothy groaned. 'Did you make it?'

Clara shook her head. 'I know I moan how much work I get, but Shelly hasn't lumbered me with the lunch duties and cleaning the clinic yet. June takes care of all that, you'll meet her soon enough.

'You did great with Eileen.' Her change of subject went unacknowledged for a moment or two, Timothy sensing this was hard for her. Flinging some crumbs, they watched for a moment as the ever-hungry galahs who had been hungrily watching them bravely swooped out of the trees and devoured their im-promptu feast.

'Look how close they come,' Timothy sighed. 'I wish I'd brought my camera.'

'They're practically tame,' Clara said, 'I feed them all the time.' Her voice grew serious. 'I meant what I said about Eileen—I mean, I don't think I could have changed her mind and I know Ross has tried...'

'Look, thanks for the vote of confidence,' Timothy said modestly, 'but I really don't think her change of heart had anything to with me. It was more a timing thing.'

'Perhaps,' Clara admitted, 'but you really were great with her.'

'Because I'm not close to her, it makes it a lot easier to be objective. And don't put yourself down. It was you she wanted to see and I don't doubt for a second it will be you doing most of the legwork if she does go ahead with the treatment.'

Clara nodded. 'I know she'll have to go to Adelaide for the radiation treatment and the surgery but Ross says that she can have the chemo at home this time—it will make all the difference.'

'It's a lot of work for you, though.'

Clara shrugged. 'I'm used to it. And it really isn't that much extra work. I just have to go and set it up. It's a small syringe driver that delivers the drug in a measured dose, so she can have it strapped to her and she can walk around with it, do the housework, whatever. I just hope she doesn't get so sick this time. That's if she decides to go ahead.'

'Let's just wait and see, huh?' The galahs had finished feeding now, fluttering back to the treetops and eyeing the visitors suspiciously. 'People and emotions I can deal with,' Timothy sighed. 'I'm just dreading a big emergency, especially somewhere like here…'

'You'd be fine,' Clara said assuredly, but Timothy just let out a long sigh.

'Doesn't anything scare you, Clara? You just seem so calm about everything. I sometimes wonder if I'll ever be that assured.'

'Of course you will be. It's just experience. Mind you, I still go cold when there's a car crash. We had a big one here a few weeks back.'

'The bus crash?' Timothy checked as Clara nodded. 'I saw it on the news.'

'It was awful.' Taking a sip of her water, she fiddled with the water bottle for a moment or two before carrying on. 'That's how my parents were killed.'

The silence around them was loaded. She could feel his eyes on her, knew that he was waiting for her to elaborate.

'Their injuries weren't that bad?' Looking up, she registered the confusion in his eyes. 'If medical help had been nearby, they'd both have lived. Mum had a pneumothorax, a chest tube would have saved her, and Dad had internal bleeding. By the time the Flying Doctors arrived it was too late.'

'Is that why you went into nursing?'

Clara nodded. 'Not for a few years after the event, though. I was only fifteen when it happened but, as Mum said, I was always going on forty.' Clara grinned, but her eyes were shining with tears as she explained. 'I was always a really sensible kid, so it wasn't hard to buckle down and concentrate on my schoolwork to get the grades for uni.'

'Who looked after you after they died?' Timothy asked. 'Have you got a lot of family?'

Clara shook her head. 'There was only me. I've got an aunt in Melbourne who said I could stay with her, she's got loads of kids and she said that one more wouldn't make a difference—in the nicest possible way,' she added, registering Timothy's taken-aback expression. 'But I couldn't bear the thought of leaving everyone and everything I knew, so I decided to stay here.'

'On your own?' He couldn't keep the shock from his voice but Clara just shook her head.

'I wasn't on my own for five minutes.' Clara smiled. 'It's like one big extended family here. I stayed with Bill and his wife for a while after it first happened and they were great, they always have been. Then when I was ready I moved back home, but I was never left alone, everyone pitched in.' She gave a soft laugh. 'I don't think I cooked a single dinner for two years.' Standing, she shook out the rug, the conversation definitely over, but Timothy knew there was a lot of hurt there, a lot more to be said.

He didn't push it.

*   *   *

'I've come for the empties!' A rather shrill voice pierced the clinic as Clara finished the restock.

'Thanks, June.' Clara smiled, handing the elderly lady the empty Esky. 'Lunch was lovely. I've left a note on the fridge for next week's mobile clinic roster. And a word of advice—if you see Timothy's name down, make an extra round of sandwiches, he eats like a horse.'

'Who eats like a horse?' Timothy grinned, a bar of chocolate and a can of cola in hand as he made his way over.

'Timothy, this is June.' Clara introduced them, expecting Timothy to impart a brief nod or a quick handshake. 'June makes the lunches and cleans the clinic.'

'The magic fairy that comes in at night?' Timothy said, putting down his can and shaking June's hand warmly. 'I was saying to Clara today that that was the best picnic I've ever tasted.'

'He was, too,' Clara agreed, smiling to herself as June blushed and patted her heavily sprayed curls.

'What was that relish in the sandwiches?' Timothy continued, food clearly one of his favourite topics.

'My own onion jam.' June gave a conspiratory wink. 'It just adds that little something extra.'

'It certainly does,' Timothy agreed.

'The recipe's been passed down in my family for generations,' June gushed. 'But I'm sure I could rustle up a jar just for you, Doctor, seeing as you're so partial to it.'

'That would be great.' Timothy grinned. 'And none of this ''Doctor'' business, it's Timothy.'

'Timothy,' June purred, tying on her pinny. 'Right, then, I'd better get started.'

'Did I hear right?' Ross's jaw was practically on the floor as he made his way over. 'You've managed to score a whole jar of June's onion jam? Shelly and I have been dropping hints for months. How about you, Clara?'

'Same here.' Clara grinned. 'I'll have to come over to yours for dinner one night, Timothy, if you've got your own stock of the contraband.'

'Any time.' For a tiny second their eyes locked, and June's blush paled into insignificance as Clara turned purple.

'About five o'clock, then.' Ross smiled as a suddenly confused Clara fumbled for her bag and headed for the door. 'Kell doesn't want a big fuss, just a few steaks on the barby at ours is all I could get him to agree to.'

'Sure.' Clara nodded, glancing at her watch and racing towards the door, determined to catch the last ten minutes of her soap. 'I've just told Shelly that I'll bring the dessert, but remind her of that, Ross, when she's panicking later—she always does way too much food.'

'We'll see you there?' Ross checked with Timothy, as Shelly came over, smothering a yawn as she pulled out the keys ready to lock up on another day.

'Great.' Heading for the door, Timothy turned around. 'How much should I put in?' As Ross frowned Timothy elaborated. 'For the present.'

'Oh, no.' Ross's frown faded as he waved him off. 'You've barely met the guy, so we don't expect you to chip in for his leaving present.'

But Timothy wasn't going anywhere.

His eyes narrowing, he eyed Ross for a moment or two before continuing. 'I meant for Clara's birthday

present.' Those green eyes weren't smiling as he took
in their horrified expressions. 'I thought as much—
you really have forgotten, haven't you? Do you realise that Eileen Benton remembered? She's been diagnosed with secondary cancer yet she still managed
to make a present and wrap it up and remembered to
wish Clara happy birthday!'

His eyes moved to the window, to Clara hurrying
past, her red hair bright in the afternoon sun, and a
smile softened his unusually harsh features as Ross
and Shelly stood there, shamed by their own thoughtlessness and stunned at the emotional outburst from
the happy-go-lucky new doctor!

'You know, guys, what attracted me to this place
when I saw the advert for the job was the *supposed*
"close knit community." Well here's a bit of free
advice—drop that stitch and the whole place will un-
ravel.'

Turning to go, Timothy changed his mind. 'And
while I'm making myself unpopular, I might as well
get everything off of my chest. Do you know there's
nothing more annoying than being told that just because you don't have children you can't possibly
know how much life hurts? Eileen Benton is Clara's
best friend. Clara was her bridesmaid, she delivered
her babies, and nursing her is hurting Clara like you
wouldn't believe. But then again, how would you
guys know? I'm sure you never thought to ask.'

The knocking on her front door didn't come as any
surprise.

People always knocked at Clara's door. Whether it
was for a cup of sugar or a wound dressing change
because the clinic was closed, Clara was used to hear-

ing a quick rap on her front door before it was pushed open and the familiar Australian greeting 'G'day' echoed down the hall.

Only this time the heavy knocking on the door wasn't followed up with footsteps, just a long pause before it started again.

'It's open,' Clara shouted loudly, her hair still dripping from her shower, a baggy T-shirt skimming her thighs as she eyed the mountain of clothes that lay in a higgledy-piggledy pile on her bed. She wished that the jumble of T-shirts and shorts and occasional shirt could somehow transform themselves into something that looked even remotely sexy.

'In here,' Clara called again as the knocking continued. Picking up a rather sheer lilac top she had bought eons ago, she hastily shoved it under her pillow. Sexy it might be—she'd bought it from a mail-order catalogue in a fit of madness—but there wasn't exactly much call for see-through lilac organza in Tennengarrah.

Realising she was actually going to have to answer the blessed door, Clara let out a small sigh, tore herself away from her rather limited wardrobe and padded barefoot along the polished floorboards of her hallway

The knocking on the door mightn't have been a surprise but the sight of Timothy Morgan standing in her doorway, hand poised ready to knock again, most certainly was.

'Didn't you hear me?' Clara remonstrated, blushing furiously as she pulled her oversized T-shirt down over her oversized bottom and gestured him to come in. 'I said it was open.'

'I heard you,' Timothy mumbled, and if Clara

hadn't known better she could have sworn that he, too, was blushing as he followed her through to the lounge. 'But it didn't seem right just to barge in. I thought perhaps you were expecting someone. I didn't want to startle you.'

'You didn't,' Clara lied, waiting for Timothy to tell her what he wanted, to explain why he was here, but when nothing was forthcoming, ever practical, Clara got straight to the point.

'What can I help you with?'

'Help me with?' Timothy gave her a slightly startled look. 'Nothing. I just came to walk you over to the barby.'

'Oh.'

'I thought it might make things a bit easier for you if you had someone to go with.'

'Oh.' Not the wittiest of responses but it was the best she could do. 'I'm just getting dressed. Can I get you a drink or anything?'

'No, thanks.' He gave a nervous smile. 'I'll just wait here, shall I?'

Clara nodded, her smile equally nervous. 'I shan't be long. Make yourself at home.'

Sitting himself on the edge of the sofa, Timothy looked around, taking in the heavy wooden furniture, the clutter of framed photos on every available surface, the worn rug on the wooden floorboards. It didn't look like an independent, just on thirty, woman's home and if he hadn't known better he wouldn't have been surprised if Mr and Mrs Watts had strolled into the lounge to assess Clara's escort for the evening!

But despite the fact it was clearly a family home, neither was it a shrine to her parents. A few bright cushions broke the rather bland colour scheme, a DVD and impressive music system filled the entertainment cabinet and a pile of glossy magazines littered the coffee-table.

It was just too big.

Too big for her to be alone in.

A lump in his throat expanded like bread in water as he imagined Clara at fifteen, here in this very lounge, confused and alone, struggling to comprehend the cruel hand the world had dealt her.

'You didn't have to sit staring at the wall,' Clara admonished as she walked in. 'You should have put the television on or some music or something.' She was moving quickly, straightening magazines and trying desperately not to meet his eyes, awkward and exposed as the lilac organza made its first debut, not quite meeting the waistband or hipband or whatever it was you called it on the way too skimpy denim shorts that Clara was positive she was way too old for.

'You look fabulous,' Timothy enthused, catching her wrist as she rushed past and standing up beside her. 'Is this a last-ditch effort to make Kell realise what he could be missing out on?'

She started to laugh, even opened her mouth to lightheartedly agree, but somewhere midway she changed her mind. His hand was hot and dry around her wrist, she could feel her radial pulse flickering against the fleshy nub of his thumb, and as her eyes met his the confusion that flickered could easily have been misinterpreted for something that looked suspiciously like lust.

'No,' she said slowly, her voice coming out more breathlessly than she'd intended. She cleared her

throat as she retrieved her wrist before heading off to
the kitchen to collect the dessert she had promised
Shelly. Resting her burning cheeks against the cool
white kitchen tiles, she ran a steadying hand across
her rarely exposed midriff, concentrating on slowing
her breathing down as she contemplated the shift in
her feelings, the revelation that utterly astounded her.

'I'm doing this for me.'

CHAPTER FIVE

IT SHOULD have been the worst day of her life.

Should have been hell on earth, saying goodbye to Kell and to all her secretly harboured dreams.

But somehow, with Timothy by her side, with his arm slung casually over her shoulders as they sidled up to the barby and handed over a bottle of wine and the huge Pavlova Clara had made, it wasn't as agonising as she had thought it would be.

It wasn't agony at all, in fact.

Ross and Shelly fell on her the second she arrived, plying her with some champagne as a cake appeared with rather too many candles twinkling away.

'You didn't have to do all this,' Clara said shyly, as everyone crowded around and belted out 'Happy Birthday.' 'It's no big deal.'

'It's a very big deal,' Shelly said, thrusting a massive bottle of perfume into her hands and giving her a kiss on the cheek, her sparkling eyes guiltily catching Timothy's for a small second.

Even when Kell took her to one side and told her she was the best friend a guy could wish for and gave her a glimpse of the engagement ring. Clara managed a genuine smile and a kiss on the cheek for luck, and actually meant it when she wished him well, wished him and Abby all the love in the world.

'It's all right,' Clara mumbled, as she made her way back to Timothy who was trying to look as if wasn't watching. 'I didn't say anything out of place—

you don't have to slam me up against a wall and start kissing me again.'

'Shame.' Timothy laughed, 'I rather enjoyed that.' His voice grew more serious. 'How was it?'

'It was OK, believe it or not.' Clara blinked. 'Mind you, I think it helped that I didn't like the ring he'd chosen—Argyle diamonds really aren't my thing.'

'You didn't tell him that?' Timothy yelped.

'Of course not. I told him it was beautiful, that Abby would love it, all the sort of things that a good friend would say.' The slight break in her voice didn't go unnoticed and Timothy eyed her with concern.

'Time we were out of here, I think.'

'It will look rude,' Clara protested. 'I should offer to help Shelly clear up afterwards.' But it was a half-hearted effort and when Timothy started on the round of goodbyes she joined in, grateful for his foresight as tears grew alarmingly close at the final hurdle and Kell pulled her in for a final goodbye hug.

'Come on, you,' Timothy said when finally it was over. 'Let's get you home.'

They walked back in silence. Shooting a look sideways at him, she watched as Timothy pretended to be intrigued with the miles of empty road ahead and a smile played on the edge of her lips.

'I'm all right,' she ventured. 'You are allowed to talk to me, you know.'

'I was trying to give you some space.'

'Well, you don't have to,' Clara replied. 'I'm fine. More than fine, in fact, I'm not even crying.'

'You did really well.'

'It wasn't all that hard in the end,' Clara admitted. 'I guess at the end of the day I'm happy for him.'

'Still hurts, though.' They were at her door now, and Clara turned to face him.

'Not that much, at least not as much as it would have if I'd made a complete fool of myself on Saturday night.'

'You wouldn't have made a fool of yourself,' Timothy argued, and Clara let out an incredulous laugh.

'Oh, come on, Timothy, of course I would have. That's why you stopped me, remember?'

He stared at her then, really stared, his mouth opening to speak then closing again, but Clara filled the gap for him.

'I'd have looked like an idiot... I'd have looked...'

'Clara.' Something in his voice stilled her, and when she looked up something in his eyes told her he meant business. 'I stopped you from telling Kell how you felt because I could see how awkwardly things might have ended up. But never, not even for a moment did I think that you'd have looked silly.' One hand cupped her cheek and she found herself staring back at him, her eyes trapped like those of a rabbit caught in the headlights. 'You would never have looked like a fool,' he said more forcibly, 'because any guy in their right mind would be glad to hear it from someone as gorgeous as you. I just didn't want to see you get hurt.'

He was fumbling in his pocket now and Clara couldn't be positive but she was sure she could see the beginning of a blush darken his cheeks as he pulled out a small box from his shorts. 'They're not quite Argyle diamonds, I'm afraid.'

Bemused, she opened the small navy box he offered, staring dumbly at the two small earrings twinkling back at her.

'They're opals,' he offered needlessly, when Clara didn't say anything. 'If you get out a magnifying glass, of course. I found them when I was fossicking in Coober Pedey, and I had them made into earrings.'

'They're beautiful,' Clara murmured, snapping the small box closed and handing them back.

'They're yours,' Timothy said shyly. 'Happy birthday, Clara.'

'Don't be ridiculous.' Her hand was outstretched but Timothy wouldn't take them back. 'I can't take them, Timothy. We both know that you had these made for your blonde nurse…Rhonda, isn't it?'

'It is and I did,' Timothy said slowly, 'but I'd say you're rather more deserving, and anyway I've got an ulterior motive.' He gave her the benefit of his lovely smile. 'Their colour changes, depending on the mood of the wearer. So next time I think you're furious with me I can sneak a look at the stones and know that you're just premenstrual or whatever.' He watched a smile creep across her face, watched as she opened the box again, her eyes staring in wonder at the small opals glittering back at her. 'What colour are they now?'

'Turquoise,' Clara said breathlessly, 'with tiny flashes of red.'

'You know what that means, don't you?' he whispered, his lips moving towards hers for the second time since their recent first meeting. 'Maybe you do like me after all.' Only this time his movements were unhurried, this time she had every chance to escape, every chance to call things off. There was no barn wall to lean against, nothing holding her up other than an arm that moved around her waist, steadily pulling her in, and even though this kiss was a world away from the one they had shared, even though this kiss was loaded with emotion and tenderness, there was a heady familiarity about it, a delicious sense of rightness as she revisited that unique masculine smell, the quiet strength of arms that held her, the rough scratch of his jaw mingling with the soft sweet fruit of his lips and the cool heady feel of his tongue. And somewhere in mid-kiss, somewhere mid-breath, her eyes opened, realisation dawning, and she pulled away startled, but still he smiled, still he held her, still he adored her with his eyes.

'I'm sorry.'

'I thought we were going to stop apologising.'

'I—I am, w-we are,' she stammered, her eyes darting over his shoulder and catching sight of the gathered crowd in the distance at Ross and Shelly's, terrified how much she had enjoyed kissing Timothy and feeling strangely disloyal to the adoration she had, till so recently, felt for Kell.

'Don't look at Kell,' he whispered, pulling her hand up to his chest, 'Here, feel, I'm real Clara. Not some fantasy, not some distant dream you've got into your head.'

'It just seems wrong.' She turned her troubled eyes to him. 'Yesterday—'

'Forget yesterday.' Timothy implored. 'Clara, we both know we're attracted to each other.'

She nodded slowly. It would have been stupid to deny it with a heart rate topping a hundred and lips still tingling from his kiss.

'But what if you're a rebound? What if—?'

'We'll be each other's rebounds,' Timothy whispered. 'We'll massage each other's bruised egos and have three delicious months together, spoiling each other and inflating each others egos till we both think we're gorgeous.'

'I'm scared,' Clara admitted, 'scared of being hurt again.'

'No one's going to get hurt,' Timothy whispered, 'because we know the rules from the start. I'm going to be gone in three months, you're going to stay here. And that's OK. We've both got different goals, different lives to lead. But we can still make this the best three months of our lives, still make each day count.'

'It's not that easy,' Clara argued. 'Look at Abby and Kell, look how hard it's been for them.'

'OK, then.' Timothy shrugged. 'We can work alongside each other in a state of pent-up frustration, say goodbye at the clinic each evening and carry on being lonely.'

She stared back at him, the warmth the strength he radiated seeping into her, filling her with a fresh surge of confidence and a rare glimpse at a future that might just be OK.

'Just because it isn't for ever, it doesn't mean it can't be wonderful.'

He made it sound so straightforward, made the world seem surprisingly simple all of a sudden. Live for today, to hell with the consequences, just lean on each other for however much time they had. As she pushed her front door open and he followed her inside, Clara was assailed by a sudden sense of freedom, an empowering surge of adrenaline as for the first time in her adult life she acted on impulse and let her heart lead the way and finally lived for the moment.

'No regrets in the morning,' Timothy checked as Clara shook her head.

'No regrets.'

'You're gorgeous,' he enthused, barely closing the door as he ravaged her again. He made her feel beautiful, made her feel every bit as sexy as one of the stunning models in a magazine, as divine as one of the blonde seductive soap stars that graced her television every evening. The way he kissed her, held her, adored her, rippled through her dented pride, soothing away the hurt, the pain she had learnt to live with for so long now. Only when they made it to the bedroom did she start to panic.

Somehow she had expected some restraint, for the infamous English reserve to rear its head, but despite his impeccable manners at work, despite his usual politeness to all and sundry, in the bedroom it would seem Timothy didn't possess even an ounce of modesty. Instead, he was undressing with lightning speed, almost falling over as he pulled off his boots such was his haste to get back to her.

More worrying than that, though, was the fact that naked he was gorgeous.

Seriously gorgeous.

Which would have been a bonus, of course, if she didn't feel like a beached whale in comparison!

Some men really are better undressed and, as divine as he looked with clothes on, seeing him in all his naked glory had Clara's confidence plummeting like a lift with the cable snapped. His body was perfectly toned, the honey brown hair only applied to his head. His legs, arms and chest were gently brushed with golden blonde, courtesy of the hot Australian sun. And the only bit the sun hadn't seen wasn't being particularly shy either, begging her to come closer, transfixing her to the spot as she eyed his delicious length. And Clara wished like she had never wished before that she were a tenth as beautiful as Timothy. Wished the sun didn't ravish her body with a million freckles, wished she'd stuck to every diet and done a million sit-ups each morning. Slowly, cringing with embarrassment, she pulled off her T-shirt, wishing her sports bra wasn't quite so sensible, wishing her breasts weren't quite so big and the soft mound of hair as he pulled at her panties wasn't quite so, well, ginger! But she could hardly ask the hairdresser for foils down there and, given the fact it was still only seven p.m. and the lights weren't even on to switch off, all she could do was pray they'd somehow make it to bed somehow conjoined…

But Timothy was having none of it.

'I want to see you,' he murmured, moving back, peeling her reluctant hand away as she tried fruitlessly to cover herself. 'Oh, Clara…'

His moan was so thick with desire, his eyes so blazing with lust that for a second she almost believed him, for a moment, as he ran his approving eyes over her body, she actually believed she was beautiful. But nerves caught up as his scrutiny became more intense, as his hands touched one gloriously ripe breast and he lowered his head to kiss it.

'I'm too fat,' she mumbled, her hands moving to cover herself, wishing it was night-time, wishing the shutters on her window could shut out just a bit more of the bright evening light.

'Never hide yourself.' Timothy shook his head,

peeling her hands away again and slowly, slowly bending to kiss one aching pink nipple as his hand slipped between her legs, parting the golden amber until Clara moaned in pleasure, the heat of his touch, the utter admiration in his eyes finally hitting the mark until under his skilful touch she felt truly beautiful.

Slowly he laid her on the bed, kissing every last freckle, chasing away every last doubt until all she needed, wanted, craved even, was for him to fill her, so close to surrender as with one thrust he entered her, her legs coiling around his back like a reflex action, her ankles entwining as she pulled him closer, moved with him, gasped with him, gave in to him, gave in to her body, answered his urgent demands with needs of her own as they exploded together, her buttocks rising off the bed as he moved her higher, longer, deeper than Clara had ever thought possible, the blessed release of her orgasm a cleansing renewal, an unexpected but delicious liberation from the ties that had bound her for so long.

Lying in his arms, naked and spent, not even caring that the sheet lay in a crumpled heap on the floor, Clara was scarcely able to believe that her heart, which had felt so wounded, so broken, so bleeding, actually felt whole again.

Turning to face him, she frowned at the troubled expression on his face. 'W-what's wrong?' she stammered, sitting up abruptly and grabbing for the sheet, feeling twitchy and exposed all of a sudden, so sure that the bubble as usual was about to burst. 'I thought you said no regrets.'

'I did, didn't I?' Grabbing her wrist, he pulled her

back beside him, her frown fading into a gurgle of laughter as Timothy carried on talking.

'I'm just worried what Hamo's going to have to say when he finds out about us.'

CHAPTER SIX

'WHAT did she have?' Squinting at the alarm clock, Clara struggled to come to as Timothy made his way none too quietly into the bedroom, pulling off his shorts and boots in that order and wondering why he nearly toppled over.

'Both.' He grinned into the darkness as, kneeling up on the bed, Clara rubbed his tired shoulders. 'My first set of twins. Ross stayed but I did it all myself. A little boy first, he took for ever to come but the second one was over in fifteen minutes. She was breech, but there wasn't a problem.'

'I bet Rick was over the moon,' Clara commented. 'Even though he said he didn't care, I know he wanted a boy.'

'Well, he struck the jackpot with both. I'm surprised they didn't find out.'

The dizzy excitement had gone from his voice now, replaced instead with deep low tones as he relaxed under Clara's gentle touch.

'I guess when you've tried so hard to have a baby the sex doesn't really matter,' Clara said softly. 'They've been on IVF for years, which is no mean feat out here.'

'How come you weren't there?' Timothy asked. 'For the delivery, I mean. You've been so involved— I thought you'd want to see it through.'

'You've built a good rapport with Rick and Emma

and they had Ross there as well. I know how exciting delivering twins is, I figured you deserved a go.'

'And a breech to boot!'

'A night for firsts.' Clara smiled, carrying on the massage and enjoying it every bit as much as Timothy clearly was. The feel of his skin beneath her fingers, the tense balls of muscle softening as she worked them gently, moving in ever-decreasing circles along his shoulders as he rolled his neck and breathed out slowly.

'Lord, it felt good, Clara. So good, in fact, I might even give up on surgery and change to obstetrics.'

'You say that after every delivery.' Clara laughed. 'But I know what you mean. There's nothing quite like it, is there? Watching that tiny little bundle come into the world, it still gets me even after all these years.'

'It was amazing. Hey.' Reaching over, Timothy picked up a bottle. 'Look what Rick gave me—a bottle of champagne and a cigar. How about it?'

'Yes to the champagne.' Clara smiled, enjoying his euphoria. 'But if you light up in here, you're sleeping alone.'

'Fair enough.' He popped the cork in a second, didn't even bother to get glasses, and never had the world seemed so great, lying in bed sipping icy champagne out of the bottle with a man as divine as Timothy. 'Do you know what I fancy?' Timothy asked, handing her the bottle. 'The biggest slab of pizza.'

'We're not in London,' Clara pointed out, levering herself out of the bed. 'The nearest I can come up with is some cheese on toast and if you're lucky a slice or two of tomato.'

'I'd rather have you.' His hand reached over and pulled her back. 'Would you find out?'

'Find out what?' Clara asked, settling back into the crook of his arm, shivering with expectancy as he ran a lazy hand along her waist.

'What you were having—if you were pregnant, I mean.'

She stilled in his arms. 'I've never really thought about it.' So deep was her blush that despite the darkness Clara was sure he must feel it radiating from her like a furnace.

She hadn't thought about it.

At least not until recently.

With Kell the fantasy had stopped at the barn. Tea lights and gardenias had been as far as she'd got, but since she'd been with Timothy suddenly all sort of ridiculous thoughts were popping into her consciousness at the most inappropriate of times.

Like now.

Imaging herself pregnant.

Imagining Timothy's euphoria.

Gurgling babies with his deep green eyes, or perhaps her blue ones topped with toffee-brown curly hair...

But not ginger.

The fantasy always pulled up short there.

'I think about it.' His clear voice filled the darkness. His honesty almost scared her. 'I think about it all the time.'

If ever there was a time when life for Clara was pretty near perfect, those first couple of months with Timothy were just about it.

He adored her.

Not just in bed, but in everything she did. And it was nice, so refreshingly nice to be a part of a couple. To have someone to come home to or someone to wait up for. To have someone ask about her day and actually listen as she rattled on about how busy the clinic was, how appallingly long the mobile clinic had taken without Kell, how insufferable it was, for all intents and purposes, to be the only nurse in an expanding clinic. Even a fleeting bout of gastro was bearable with Timothy clucking over her like a broody hen, ringing in sick for her and policing the telephone whenever Shelly rang to enquire how she was doing. Even the agony of nursing Eileen, watching her hair disappear along with her spirit, was made slightly more bearable with Timothy beside her, letting her rant about the injustice of the world or simply holding her when she wept, when it all became too much.

'Ross asked me my plans yesterday,' Timothy ventured one morning, as they waited for the third snooze alarm to finally force them out of bed. Staring into the semi-darkness, Clara didn't say anything, just pulled back the sheet and made to get up as a grumbling Timothy pulled her back to the cosy warmth of the bed.

'Come on, Clara, five more minutes—there's no rush.'

'Oh, yes, there is.' Pushing the sheet back, Clara lay for a moment willing her legs to move from the cosy warmth of Timothy's embrace. 'If I don't get a move on, I'm going to late and so will you.'

'Doesn't matter.' Timothy grinned. 'Ross told me he's already written my reference.'

It was a joke, a tiny little light-hearted comment,

but not for the first time Clara felt her heart sink further at the inevitability of Timothy's departure. Three months had stretched before them like an eternity at the start, like the beginning of the school holidays when she had been a child. Endless weeks stretching ahead, an endless summer that would surely last for ever. But it was almost over now, like the uniforms being taken out, pencil cases checked, books being labelled. A glimpse of what lay ahead had her heart sinking at the prospect…

'Just five more minutes,' Timothy grumbled. 'I'm trying to talk to you.'

'It's seven o'clock, Timothy.' Clara gestured to her small alarm clock. 'I'm supposed to be there in half an hour and I'm supposed to be doing a house call on Eileen this morning.'

'She's going to get better,' Timothy said gently, as Clara listlessly pushed the sheet back, dreading the house call she had pencilled into her diary for later that day.

'You don't know that,' Clara snarled, terrified to believe him. 'I thought doctors were supposed to err on the side of caution, be guarded in their outlooks. You can't just sit there and say she'll get better just like that. What's the point of false hope?'

'No point at all,' Timothy said evenly, refusing to rise to her outburst. 'But there is still hope for Eileen. Chemo does this, Clara, you know that better than anyone. The cure can be worse than the disease, you've got to stay positive for as long as Eileen needs you to and not a day longer.'

'So you're a psychiatrist as well as an oncologist now, are you?'

Her bitter words were so out of character with her

usual gentle nature that for a moment or two they both just stared at each other, until Timothy broke the strained silence.

'Don't shut me out, Clara. I'm here for you.'

She gave a low laugh. 'But for how long, Timothy? It's all very well for you to be positive, to have encouraged Eileen to take the treatment, to offer to be there, but you're not going to be, are you? It's me that will be left holding her hand, it's me that has to witness the kids watching their mother slowly dying. You'll be up in Queensland with your underwater camera, snapping away at the reef, so don't lie there and tell me not to shut you out when we both know that you're going anyway.'

Standing under the shower, Clara massaged shampoo into her hair, trying to ignore the memory of Timothy's hurt expression when she had left the bed.

He was only trying to help, only trying to comfort her, she knew that deep down, but therein lay the problem.

Soon he would be gone, out of her life and on to pastures new—and what then?

She'd always been independent, self-reliant, but Timothy had crept into her heart with alarming stealth, had become the rock she leant on, her hope, her sounding-board, and all too soon it was going to be taken away.

Of course she wanted him to stay, she wanted that more than anything else in the world, but she was scared, scared of telling him just how much she wanted it. Terrified of a needy note creeping into her voice, terrified of betraying to him just how much she needed him, that he was so very much more than a rebound.

They walked over to the clinic together, for once the silence between them unusually strained.

'Do you want me to talk to Ross—about staying on, I mean?'

'You do what's right for you, Timothy.'

'What about us?'

They were at the clinic door now, hardly the best place for an in-depth discussion, but Clara did her best. 'I want you to stay on. It's just…'

'Just what?'

Clara took a deep breath. 'Well, you're going to go one day, aren't you?' When he didn't say anything Clara pushed a bit harder. 'Aren't you?'

'You know I have to.'

Clara gave a small nod, not trusting herself to speak.

'There's nothing to stop you coming with me, though.'

'So my job doesn't count? I'm only a nurse all of a sudden.' She turned hurt eyes to him. 'It didn't take long for you to start pulling rank, did it?'

'That's not what I meant and you know it,' Timothy flared, but Clara refused to back down.

'I'm the only nurse here, Timothy.'

'There's Shelly.'

That didn't even merit a response. 'If I walk away now, what's going to happen? Who's going to take care of people like Eileen?'

'Ross will have to find someone else,' Timothy said evenly, and Clara gave a scoffing laugh.

'Oh, come on, Timothy, we've got a permanent ad in all the papers, we're registered with every agency in the land and still we never get anyone for more than a few months. I can't just walk away. This is my family, I have a duty to them.'

'What about your duty to yourself, Clara?' Timothy pushed, refusing to get it. 'Don't you deserve to have a life, to be happy? You don't owe Tennengarrah anything.'

But Clara refused to be swayed. The anger faded from her voice and she managed a wobbly brave smile. 'This is my home,' she said softly. 'I'm an outback girl and you're an up-and-coming surgeon. Timothy, what we've had, what we've got, it's great, but we both know…' Swallowing hard, she looked up at him. 'That this was never for ever.'

'And that's the way you want it?'

Oh, it wasn't, but it was the way it had to be so instead of speaking the truth she forced a smile. 'You've got that blonde charge nurse to get back to.'

'Oh, come on, Clara.' Timothy pulled at her hand. 'I haven't even given her a thought. What about you?'

Confused by his question, she didn't respond.

'Do you still think about Kell?

There was something in his voice she couldn't interpret, a wariness she was scared to explore.

'Clara?' His voice was sterner now, demanding a response, but Clara simply couldn't give one. Instead she pulled her hand away and walked inside. Finding shelter in the ladies' loo, she buried her face in her hands with a low moan. Screwing her eyes closed on stubborn tears, she dragged a deep breath into her body.

Kell hadn't entered her head for weeks now. It was Timothy she thought about, Timothy who demanded every second of her mind, but was that what he wanted to hear? That the rebound had misfired? That the love and devotion she had felt for Kell didn't come close to the feelings she had for him?

And suppose she did tell him, suppose she took the biggest gamble of her life and laid it all on the line, where could it possibly lead? He might adore her, want her, but he certainly didn't need her.

Timothy was going to be a surgeon while she was a true Tennengarrah girl. The rules had been laid down at the start—it was she who had broken them.

For a second she wavered. Toyed with the idea of going with him, exploring Australia, taking a diving course, following her heart...

Prolonging the agony.

And it would be agony, Clara realised, pulling off a wad of loo roll and blowing her nose loudly. Because one day his visa would run out, one day the dream would have to end, and far worse than the hurt she felt now, far worse than the confusion in his eyes she had witnessed this morning, would be the pity.

The pity in his eyes when she told him she loved him.

'Where's Ross?' Walking out of the loo, she looked around the empty clinic, frowning at Timothy's be-mused expression.

'I don't know.' Timothy shrugged. 'There's no one here.'

'But he has to be here.' Pushing open the staffroom door, Clara peered inside as Timothy caught up with her.

'He isn't. I've checked everywhere.'

'The door was open.' Clara frowned. 'Ross would never leave it unlocked, never.'

'Maybe there was an emergency,' Timothy suggested, but Clara shook her head firmly, a gnawing
bubble of panic starting to well inside her throat.

'There's often an emergency,' Clara countered, her
heat skittering into a gallop as she eyed the clinic
again, pushing doors open and calling out his name
before turning back to Timothy. 'But Ross always
locks up behind himself, it's second nature.' Running
over to the drug cupboard, she fumbled with her keys
and wrenched it open, shaking her head at the neat
boxes staring back at her, everything in its place just
as it should be. 'We haven't been robbed.'

'Maybe he got a call-out, maybe—' The sound of
footsteps running towards them had them both letting
out a mutual sighs of relief, grins appearing as Ross
bounded into the clinic.

But their relief was short-lived.

One look at his grey, angst-ridden face had Clara's
heart spinning into free fall, her usually steady hands
trembling as she reached out to her colleague, her
voice shaking. 'Ross, what on earth's happened?'

Oh, she tried to stay impassive, tried to put on her
best calm expression as Ross's terrified eyes met hers,
but even before he'd finished speaking a small wail
of horror escaped Clara's lips.

'It's Matthew.' She could hear the terror in his
voice as he said his son's name, the fear, the panic
all rolled into one as this normal weekday suddenly
exploded into a nightmare, as everything safe and
good was swept from under them. 'He's gone missing.'

CHAPTER SEVEN

STRANGE who performed in a crisis.

Such an irrelevant thought, but as Clara stood there, momentarily stunned, as Ross physically crumpled, she watched in grateful awe as Timothy took over. The most junior, the most inexperienced of all of them snapped into leader mode in an instant. His friendly, open face strong, his steps purposeful as he walked over to Ross and in clear uncompromising tones demanded answers to the questions he rapidly fired.

'When did you last see him?'

'Midnight.' Ross was sobbing openly now. 'We checked them before we went to bed. Normally Shelly goes in before her shower but Abby rang this morning—'

'Forget that.' Timothy dragged him away from ir- relevancies. 'When did you realise he was missing?'

'Shelly rang.' Ross balled his fists into his eyes, forcing deep breaths into his lungs in an effort to hold it all together. 'Maybe ten, fifteen minutes ago.'

'Have you called the police?'

Ross nodded, but the panic in his voice reached hysterical proportions as he continued. 'But Jack's two hours away, there's some campers trespassing over at Winnycreek…'

'He's coming, though,' Timothy checked, almost shaking Ross as he forced his attention. 'And did he say he was calling in help?' A small nod was the only answer Timothy got, but he turned his attention to June, who had burst through the doors, a wide smile on her face as she saw her permanently hungry young doctor coming towards her.

'June.' Timothy's voice was incredibly calm. Taking the bemused woman's hands, he spoke in low tones. 'Matthew has gone missing.' As she started to whimper he gripped her hands tighter and Clara watched as he gave the terrified woman instructions. 'I need you to stay calm, I need you to go and knock on every door you can think of and get someone to do a ring around. I want everyone who can help at the clinic, CFA members, anyone with a Jeep, a plane—do you understand?' He didn't wait for an answer and as June scuttled off he addressed Ross.

'Go back to the house.'

'I have to look—'

'Look again through the house and the garden,' Timothy broke in. 'Look in every cupboard, under every bed, every shed—he's likely to be close by. And then report back here in half an hour. But you have to keep looking. Is there anywhere you can think he might have wandered to, anywhere?' Ross shook his head, fear turning to anger as hopelessness took over, as Timothy pushed harder. 'Come on, Ross. Is there anywhere you can think of?'

'He doesn't go anywhere on his own. For heaven's sake, he's three years old, he's got Down's syndrome, he wouldn't know how to cross a road!'

'Ross.' Finally Clara found her voice, and on legs that felt like jelly she led Ross to the clinic door. 'Do what Timothy's saying, go and look with Shelly.'

As Ross raced towards the house Clara ran a shaking hand through her hair, willing herself to stay calm, to think, to form some sort of plan.

'We're going to find him.'

'Oh, and you know that too, do you?' Her tear-streaked face turned to him. 'It's going to be forty degrees today, Timothy. A little boy on his own in the outback won't last a morning. There's dingoes, snakes, dams—that's if the heat doesn't kill him first.'

'We're going to find him.' Not for a second did his voice waver, the optimism in his voice so strong Clara almost believed him. 'But we have to all pull together.'

And pull together they did.

The whole of Tennengarrah poured into the high street, all determined to play their parts, all determined to bring a special little boy home. Bruce setting off in his plane before the first trestle table had been hoisted up, clipboards appearing, maps spread out, the CFA volunteers pulling on their orange uniforms as they pored over the maps, chewing on cigarettes as they formed a plan, shouted orders, organised groups and gave out whistles.

Timothy was in charge for now, and every one knew it. Mike, the aboriginal medicine man, appeared with a group of his men, ready to share their knowledge of the bush, to utilise their tracking skills and search for clues in their own unique way. And though Timothy had only been there a relative five minutes, though his knowledge of the land was minuscule, it was him they all deferred to, him they all ran their plans by. A leader was needed and Timothy filled the part, his crisp English accent authoritative, his manners impeccable as he thanked everyone profusely, no matter how small their contribution—even the cup of tea a tearful June pressed into his hands got the same polite, grateful response. Even Hamo, Timothy's unofficial arch-enemy, bordered on approachable as he handed Timothy a fluorescent jacket and told him to put on the hard red hat. Timothy did so without comment, but the gesture didn't go unnoticed by Clara who chose that moment to slip back to the clinic.

'Where have you been?' Timothy pulled her aside the second she emerged again. 'Everyone's ready to head off.'

'I've just set up a bed for him, turned up the ice machine, set up some fans…' Registering his frown, Clara realised that, despite his air of authority, despite the leadership he was showing, this was uncharted territory for Timothy and she patiently explained her movements. 'Unless he's found in the next hour or so, Matthew's likely to be suffering from heat exhaustion. A couple of degrees centigrade either way will be the difference between survival and death, between walking away unscathed or brain damage. Our first priority will be to cool him. I was just making sure everything was ready.'

She watched as Timothy put his hands up to shield his eyes, squinting at the morning sun only just starting to show its bite, and almost felt the surge of fear that engulfed him, registered a nervous swallow as he turned to the gathered crowd.

'Let's get moving,' Timothy called above the anxious chatter, demanding attention, which he respectfully received. 'Now, remember, only search the area you've been allocated. When you're sure it's clear, come back and Hamo will brief you again. We have to keep in touch.'

'Ross is coming.' The hope in Clara's voice faded as his ashen face came into view.

'You go to Shelly,' Timothy said firmly.

'I should be searching,' Clara argued. 'I know the land like the back of my hand.'

'So do most of the locals,' Timothy pointed out. 'But Shelly needs you now. You need to keep her calm, let her ramble if she wants to, but anything she says, no matter how small, if you think there's a clue there, let me know.'

Clara nodded. Turning to go, she swung back around and for a second, despite the hub of activity, despite the crowd that surrounded them, it was as if only the two of them were there. 'He'll be OK, won't he?' As contrary as her words sounded, as furious as she'd been at him for his blind optimism, suddenly it was everything Clara needed, hope to cling to as she faced Matthew's mother, strength to feed from as she dealt with the agony ahead.

A tiny smile softened his features for a second.

'He's going to be fine,' Timothy said softly, before turning back to the crowd, back to the search teams he had organised, back to the people who also needed his quiet strength.

Shelly didn't even look up as Clara slipped quietly inside. Trapped in her own private hell, she sat on the edge of the sofa, staring unblinkingly at a tattered book she held in her hands as Clara sat beside her.

There was silence for a moment or two before Shelly finally spoke.

'It's his favorite book.' Shelly ran her finger over the cover. 'You've no idea how many times I've read it to him. He gave it to Kate when she was born, but he still sneaks it out of her bookcase every night for me to read, then he insists that I put it back.

'He's going to be OK, isn't he, Clara? They'll find him, won't they?'

And though she had seen Ross's agony, though she had seen fear and pain in more patients than she could truthfully remember, as Shelly dragged her eyes to Clara, Clara witnessed there and then the utter devastation of her friend, and she felt grateful, so grateful for Timothy's optimism, for the ray of hope she could offer. Even if it was a false promise, even though the answer couldn't possibly be known, now wasn't the time to take hope away.

'He's going to all right.' Clara took one of Shelly's cold hands and held it tightly. 'Everyone's out there, looking for him, and they're going to find him, Shelly.'

'I should have looked in on him first thing. I always do,' Shelly sobbed. 'But Abby rang, and I was just so grateful the kids were still asleep so I could have a proper chat, and all that time—'

'You did nothing wrong,' Clara said firmly. 'This isn't your fault.'

'Oh, it is.' Shelly was inconsolable. Used to grief, Clara let her talk, let Shelly voice her fears as she herself sat quietly holding Shelly's hand.

'His whole little world has changed since Kate came along. He's so much more clingy and jealous, and I tried to give him more time, tried to be there for him, but there was always something going on, always a shift that needed to be filled...'

'Oh, Shelly.' Tears brimmed in Clara's eyes as she watched her friend and colleague struggle just to remember to breathe, and only then did Clara realise that Shelly's supposed insensitivity at times had nothing to do with her. Shelly was another mum battling to do it all, to somehow find enough hours in the day. 'I'm sorry. If I'd known, I'd have done more.'

'You couldn't have done any more.' Shelly shook her head. 'You do too much already. Abby rang this morning, she said she had some great news and she sounded so happy, so excited that for a second I thought they were coming back, that we'd finally have more staff and I could stay home with the kids. But she told me they were getting married and instead of being happy for them I was disappointed. What sort of person does that make me?'

'Normal.' Clara wrapped her arm around Shelly's heaving shoulders. 'Everyone misses them, and though we're thrilled they're happy it doesn't mean we can't be disappointed that they're gone.'

'Matthew misses Kell.' Shelly gave a soft laugh. 'He used to make Matthew laugh, called him "big guy" and played hide and seek with him. Kell would know where to look, he'd know what to do.' Her voice was rising, panic overriding sense now.

It was the longest morning of her life.

Like a pendulum Shelly swung between hopelessness and despair, bursts of manic laughter as she recalled some of Matthew's more endearing traits countered almost immediately with rasping, desperate hopeless tears as Clara fought to comfort her, to somehow be a friend and a professional, to hold out hope yet attempt to face the truth. The minutes that had dragged by suddenly started to gallop, the cool crisp morning evaporating. She tried to ignore the searing heat and its effect on a three-year-old boy dressed in a pair of pyjama bottoms.

'We should ring Kell.' Shelly's voice was firm. Standing, she started to pace as Clara sat quietly on the sofa. 'He might know what to do, where to look.' Shelly's eyes were wide. She was grasping at straws perhaps, but a shred of hope was better than none at all. 'We have to ring Kell.'

Clara hesitated, momentarily torn, not wanting to head down the wrong path, indulge Shelly's whims only to see her dejected and spent when deep down she was sure Kell could offer no better solutions than the ones already in better in place. And yet…

Kell had been close to Matthew, Clara realised with mounting excitement. During the last few weeks of Shelly's pregnancy Kell had often turned up at the clinic with Matthew, giving him a few crayons to draw with as he himself got on with the work, taking him for walks during his breaks. Hope started to flare. Clara rushed into the hall. Maybe Kell could offer some insight, could perhaps suggest something they hadn't already thought of.

With Shelly watching like a hawk, wringing her hands with frustration, begging her to hurry up, Clara rang the number, cursing inwardly at the recorded message.

'It's an answering-machine,' Clara said helplessly. 'He must be at work.'

She left a brief message, urging him to ring the second he returned. Shelly started pulling out phone books, frantically searching for numbers.

'Ring him at the hospital—I'm sure he's working with Abby.'

It took an age to get through, the switchboard messing up the connection, the emergency ward redirecting her twice, and if the answering-machine message had been cold and impersonal it was nothing compared to the haughty voice Clara encountered that told her Kell Bevan couldn't possibly come to the telephone right now.

'You don't understand,' Clara begged. 'This is an emergency.'

'Which is exactly what Mr Bevan is dealing with,' came the impassive response. 'I'll pass on your message as soon as he's available.'

Shelly was inconsolable. As fruitless as the call might have been, it had offered her hope, something to cling to, something to focus on, and now that it was gone. Now there really was nothing she could do she seemed to crumple before Clara's eyes. Even though she knew emotion was good, that it was better out than in, as Shelly's screams echoed through the house, as baby Kate awoke demanding attention, oblivious to the hell around her, Clara toyed with the idea of sedating Shelly just to restore some sense of order. Instead, she left her momentarily, picking up Kate, hot and angry at having been left so long, and changing her nappy, praying Shelly might settle, would hold it together for just a little bit longer.

'She's hungry.' Clara bought the wailing infant through to the lounge, deliberately ignoring Shelly's agitation, determinedly talking normally. 'She needs to be fed.'

With infinite relief she watched as Shelly checked herself, and though Clara's heart ached for Shelly she kept her voice matter-of-fact. 'Sit down, Shelly, and feed her.'

Mercifully she obeyed, little Kate latching on and sucking hungrily as Shelly kissed the soft blonde down of her baby's head, breathing in her sweet baby scent as if it was the life force she depended on, the one life raft she could cling to in this awful turbulent time.

'I forgot your birthday.' Looking down at her baby, Shelly's voice was a tiny whisper, and though it was so irrelevant, Clara followed her thread, irrelevance far more palatable than the hell they were facing. 'You're being so nice and I've been so awful. If it hadn't been for Timothy…'

'It doesn't matter,' Clara said gently, sitting on the sofa beside her. 'You probably did me a favour—it turned out to be the best birthday ever.' Fingering the tiny opals in her ears, she finally understood. 'Shelly, stop beating yourself up. You've done nothing wrong, nothing wrong at all. I'm here for you.'

'You always have been.'

The ringing of telephone caught them both unawares. Clara jumped up first, fixing Shelly with her best version of a firm glare. 'I'll get it. You carry on feeding Kate.'

Only when she picked up the telephone did Clara realise the tension that had engulfed her. Hearing Kell's voice, so normal, so utterly oblivious to the hell on the other end of the line, had Clara momentarily lost for words. Leaning against the hall wall, she let out a long low moan, tears trickling down her cheeks when finally she spoke.

'Oh, Kell.' If only she'd turned at that moment, if only she'd registered Timothy pushing open the fly door, walking in unannounced, maybe she'd have changed her tone, rephrased her words somehow. 'If ever I needed you, it's now.'

Looking up, seeing the agony on Timothy's face,

for a second she thought the worse had happened, that he was coming with bad news.

'Where's Shelly?' Timothy's voice was barely a croak.

'Feeding Kate.'

'I'm here.' Pale and trembling, Shelly stepped forward, Kate in her arms as her terrified eyes turned to Timothy. 'Have you found him?'

So devastated was his expression that when Timothy shook his head Clara almost dropped the telephone in relief, so sure had she been that the worst possible outcome had actually transpired. 'It's Kell.' Handing the phone to Shelly, she took Kate and walked through to the lounge, Timothy following a step behind.

'What you just heard,' Clara ventured as Timothy stood there, his face rigid, his eyes guarded, 'wasn't what it sounded like. Shelly was hysterical. She got it into her head that Kell might know where Matthew had gone. I was in two minds whether to sedate her—'

'It doesn't matter.' Timothy shrugged off the hand on his arm and shook his head, but then seemed to change his mind, his guarded eyes flashing with anger, 'You really think Kell's going to save the day, don't you, Clara, that Kell's going to come through for you? Well, guess what? I'm here and I'm real, not some fantasy you've got locked in your head. I'm the one dressed in fluorescent orange waterproofs when it's thirty-five degrees outside, I'm the one rallying the troops and organising search parties. Where's Kell now?' His lips snarled around the words. 'Where's Kell when you need him, Clara?'

CHAPTER EIGHT

IT WAS probably a matter of seconds but it felt like hours. Clara bit back a smart reply as Timothy suddenly relented, dragging a hand through his sodden, sweat-dampened hair as he shook his head. 'Now's not the time.' Clenching his fists, he took a deep breath. 'I'm sorry, that was uncalled-for.'

It had been uncalled-for and now most definitely wasn't the time, but as she looked at him she ached physically ached to put her hand to his taut, exhausted cheek to somehow put him right, but all that mattered here was Matthew. There would be time for that later.

'Is Jack here yet?'

Timothy nodded wearily. 'Everyone's here. The Flying Doctors just came in, Hall's checked the bed you set up and he's happy everything's ready. June's even icing sheets and boxing them up in Eskys to wrap him in the second he's found. People are coming in from all over, just wanting to help, to do something, anything. I've never seen anything like it, never seen people pull together in that way.' Sitting down, he rested his head in his hands as Clara started to pour a glass of iced water from the jug. Realising the waste in energy, she just handed him the jug which he took without comment, downing the water in one, not even wiping away the rivers that spilled onto him. Clara quietly watched, sensing his weariness, knowing the force of the harsh Australian sun while simultaneously trying not to imagine a little boy out there alone with the elements.

'Take your jacket off.'

'I have to get back.'

'Two minutes,' Clara implored, pulling the heavy jacket off as Timothy took a tiny, much-needed break. 'What does Jack say?'

'That he has to be near.' For the first time since sitting down he looked up and Clara felt like weeping when she saw the devastation in his eyes, the hopelessness of the message he imparted. 'They're bringing in the police divers, they're going to search the dams.'

'No.' She shook her head fiercely. 'He's hiding somewhere. He's just a baby, for heaven's sake, and he's going to be fine.'

'Clara.' His eyes couldn't meet hers. Instead, he stared at the empty jug in his hands, and she truly couldn't tell if it was sweat or tears that ran down his exhausted face. 'He is just a baby and this is the outback.' She watched his Adam's apple bob up and down, heard the tremor in his voice and she wanted him to take it back, to some how snap back into the wonderful optimist she'd berated before, for hope to impinge on hopelessness, but again he shook his head, 'The police are asking questions, you know the sort of questions as well as I do.'

She shook her head fiercely. 'Well, they're wrong and it's a waste of time even going through it. Their time would be better spent looking for him than heading up that path.'

But Timothy hadn't finished. 'They want to know if Shelly suffered any postnatal depression, if there's any family dynamics, any history that might point to—?'

'No.' Screwing her eyes closed, Clara took a mental swipe at him, or maybe her hands made contact. No matter how many times afterwards she relived the moment she could never be sure, but suddenly Timothy was beside her, holding her heaving shoulders and begging her to stay strong.

'We have to do this, Clara. Yes, Ross and Shelly are friends, yes, we're all close, but at the end of the day you're the nurse and I'm the doctor. When the tough talk comes, it's going to be us.'

'But it's not like that,' Clara said forcefully. 'Ross and Shelly adore him.'

Timothy nodded. 'We know that, but the police don't. They're not pointing the finger, it's just the system.'

'The system?' Jumping back, she stared at him, eyes wide, almost deranged with the preposterousness of the world. 'What does the ''system'' know about love, what does the ''system'' know about devotion? Ross isn't Matthew's biological father.' She watched as Timothy flinched. 'Can you imagine the ''system's'' response to that? I can just imagine the press with that little gem, just imagine the innuendoes, the snide little remarks, when the truth is that Ross loves Matthew more than his biological father. Ross would die before harming a hair on that child's head, so don't you stand there and tell me to be professional, don't you stand there and expect me to ask the tough questions because I won't do it, Timothy, I just won't.' Her voice trailed off as Shelly returned, but there was a determined edge to it as she turned to meet her friend. 'I'll resign here and now before I go there, Timothy. I simply won't do it.'

'Kell doesn't know where he could be.' Shelly's voice trembled as she walked towards them and Clara instinctively took Kate from her arms, sensing the desolation before them. 'They went for walks, but only along the main street. He took him to the park, to the milk bar, but apart from that he can't think of anything. They played peek-a-boo...'

'The barn.'

Timothy's voice forced their attention.

'The barn,' Timothy said again, breaking into a run.

Clara quelled the adrenaline that surged inside her and resisted running after him. Instead, she handed Kate to Shelly and forced an air of authority as her pulse pounded in her temples and instinct told her to follow.

'Shelly, wait here.'

The air was hot in her lungs, too hot to run, but nothing could have stalled her, nothing could have made her stay put as she pounded the red earth on legs that felt like jelly, her chest exploding as she followed Timothy through the town, the locals parting as they blazed a trail through the centre, oblivious of Hamo as he shouted behind them.

'We've already checked it. He isn't there.'

'He has to be here.' She watched with mounting despair as he turned over hay bales, shouting Matthews's name, prodding into the dark, damp mounds in a fruitless, hopeless last effort. 'He was playing hide and seek with Kell at the ball, climbing into empty beer kegs.'

'There are some more kegs out the back.' Hamo

frantically beat on the door, wrenching the wooden
plank that barred the back entrance as Timothy raced
through, the searing heat of the morning sun harsher
now after the relative cool of the barn.

'Matthew.'

Something in his voice stilled her.

Something told Clara it wasn't false hope that
surged inside her.

'Matthew!'

But jubilation was short-lived, joy had its downside
as Timothy pulled the flushed, limp body from an
upturned keg. Hamo rushed to smother him with one
of June's iced sheets as Timothy barely paused for
breath, pulling the cool cotton around the limp little
boy and running towards the clinic as if his own life
depended upon it. Cheers went up as the gathered
locals parted to let them through.

And Clara followed, perfecting her mental plan of
attack as she ran. Running through the town, she
begged an answer, prayed to a God that must surely
be listening that there must be a reason, some sense
to it all. That, yes, he was three, and he had Down's
syndrome. But the fact he still used a bottle at night
and had wandered off with his bottle of juice in his
hand might just have saved him.

Professionalism took over then, emotions put aside
as they laid the limp body on a gurney. Jack pulled
Ross outside and Clara, Hall and Timothy worked
together. Hall, the most senior, took the head of the
gurney, calling orders in his thick Australian accent.

'What's his temp?'

'Forty point five degrees,' Clara answered, not even
looking up as she placed ice bags around Matthew's
head, in his groin and under his arms, then filled a

burette with fluid as Timothy slapped Matthew's veins, slipped a needle in and enabled the lifesaving fluids to enter his system to hydrate the tiny body that lay on the gurney. 'But cooling started a few minutes ago, he would have been warmer when we found him.'

'Aim to cool him at point two degrees a minute,' Hall ordered.

They worked on almost in silence, Hall occasionally requesting something, but the words were barely out before his requests were met. Clara, ever efficient, the consummate professional, despite her fraught emotions, sprayed the little boy with tepid water, aiming the fans over his body.

'What about a cool bath?' Timothy asked, answering his own questions as he worked diligently on. 'Or would that be too much of a shock?'

'Evaporative cooling is the best,' Hall answered knowledgeably. 'This is the best way to get to this little tacker's temp down. Let's get some blood gases on him, Clara. Timothy, put a catheter in—we need to monitor his renal function.'

On and on they worked, trying to ignore Shelly's screams in the background, Ross's fruitless attempts to be let inside.

'What's his blood sugar?'

'Four.' Clara looked up, perhaps for the first time. 'Temp?'

'Thirty-nine point two.' For the first time she remembered to breathe again properly, watching as the tachycardia signs on the monitor over them became slightly more even, the little dry red face of Matthew grimacing as he pulled at the oxygen mask over his face, scared blue eyes opening momentarily, a fat little hand pulling at the drip in his arm, his eyebrows furrowing as he struggled to focus.

'Looks like we're winning.'

It had to be sweat. Hall was the most experienced, the most laid-back doctor Clara had even had the privilege to work with, but for just a second as Matthew tugged at the oxygen mask and four little limbs moved the way four little limbs should, as Matthew's parched, cracked lips attempted to form a word, Clara could have sworn a tear trickled down the side of Hall's sun-battered cheeks.

'Kell?' The single word was the sweetest they had ever heard, the blue eyes that gazed at Timothy like two precious jewels as Timothy shook his head, gently stroking the little boy's face as he stared down at him.

'Sorry, buddy, you'll just have to make do with me.' He made a pretty good attempt at a calm voice as he called out, 'Let Shelly and Ross in.'

But for all his strength, for all the optimism and hope he had imbued, Clara knew Timothy wouldn't come out of this turbulent time unscathed, and as she led Ross and Shelly in, as they gazed in wonder at the life that had so nearly been taken, she looked up and realised that it was the first time she had seen Timothy cry.

'He needs intensive care.' Hall's voice was gruff but there was gentleness behind it as he addressed Matthew's parents, deliberately ignoring the fact that Ross was a doctor and Shelly a nurse, knowing that now more than ever a terrified mum and dad were all they wanted to be. 'His temperature was very high when he came to us, which can cause a lot of problems, but thankfully he seems to have avoided any serious damage. Neurologically he's responding well and he's putting out urine, which are good signs. Still, I'd be happier to have him at a major centre.'

Ross looked up helplessly and Timothy responded without prompting. 'We'll manage fine, Ross—just go.'

'You'll stay at the house?' Ross checked. 'There's an emergency bell on the clinic door, it rings directly through to the house. If you leave a note people might not be able to read—'

'We'll stay at the house,' Timothy said firmly. 'Don't worry about the clinic—you just concentrate on your family, for as long as it takes. We'll be fine.'

Slinging a weary arm around Clara as the stretcher was gently loaded onto the plane, Timothy pulled her nearer. 'Won't we?'

'I hate being a grown-up,' Timothy moaned as, fed, showered and changed, he finally collapsed on Ross and Shelly's sofa. 'I've just had the most terrifying day of my life and I can't even relax with a glass of wine in case that bloody bell goes off.'

'It kind of makes you realise what Ross and Shelly have to put up with each and every night, doesn't it?' Clara said, listlessly picking up toys from the floor and piling them into a massive wooden box.

'You've changed your tune.' Timothy teased, half-heartedly pinching her on the bottom as Clara retrieved the umpteenth piece of Lego, locating a dusty toast crust along the way. 'I thought *you* were the misunderstood one.'

'I thought I was, too,' Clara admitted, giving in to the mess and plonking herself down on the sofa beside him. 'Today kind of puts things into perspective, doesn't it? I mean, dramas happen here often, and as much as I moan about the hours I put in at least when I go home I can switch off. For Ross and Shelly it's twenty-four seven. Throw in breastfeeding and a special needs child and you can see why Shelly asks me to work over—'

'Doesn't make it right, though,' Timothy said loyally, but Clara just shrugged.

'But it makes sense.'

'Things will change now.' Stretching and yawning, Clara had to wait for him to elaborate. 'I know he was beside himself, I know it was fear talking, but from the way Ross was ranting, the health department wants to watch itself. He's all for closing the clinic down unless they come to the party and organise more staff.'

'Ross would never let this place close,' Clara said assuredly, but her conviction wavered as she turned to Timothy. 'Do you really think it could come to that?'

'Who knows?' Timothy yawned. 'But Ross nearly lost his son today and Shelly's got every reason not to want to fill in shifts any more. You can't do it all yourself, Clara. It's either a part-time clinic or a hospital, not somewhere in between, and I think today might just be the catalyst. Anyway, enough. I need my bed.'

She stood first, made a half-hearted effort to haul him off the sofa.

'Carry me,' Timothy grumbled.

'Carry *me*,' Clara moaned, and then as Timothy gestured to do so she blushed furiously and changed her mind. 'Don't be daft,' she mumbled, purposefully heading for the guest bedroom. 'You'd rupture your-self.'

Sleeping in Ross and Shelly's guest room was rather like being in a hotel, without the luxury of a chocolate on the pillow and a bar fridge, of course. Climbing into bed, they plumped the pillows, admired the counterpane then lay there awkward and rigid, staring at the white ceiling and wishing the curtains closed enough to stop the annoying chink of moon-light that was filtering through.

'It won't ring,' Clara whispered, sensing Timothy's tension, though why she was keeping her voice down was anyone's guess. 'Everyone knows Ross is away. It will only go off if there's an emergency.'

'Which is exactly what I'm afraid of,' Timothy mumbled, lying rigid beside her, staring into the dark-ness with a tension that was palpable. Cuddling in beside him, she moved slightly to make room for the arm he clamped firmly around her, closing her eyes against the soft down of his chest and running her hand tentatively down the flat plane of his stomach, acknowledging the slight increase in his breathing, a low, almost inaudible moan as her hand moved ever lower.

A woman of the twenty-first century Clara certainly wasn't. Oh, she knew her own mind, was indepen-dent, but when it came to sex there was still a refresh-ing naïvety about her. She'd read all the glossies, de-voured television soaps as easily as a box of chocolates and she knew deep down that women could make the first move.

She just never had before.

It had always been Timothy who'd instigated their love-making with Clara still in a state of perpetual surprise that anyone could fancy her so much, that someone so divine could actually want her.

But tonight she knew he needed her.

Needed the sweet release their love-making brought, needed to escape from the horrors of the day, however fleetingly.

Capturing his swollen warmth in her hand, she held it for a moment, revelling in its beauty, thrilled and terrified and excited all at the same time as it sprang to life in her hands, as it responded to her gentle, tentative touch. And his obvious delight in her boldness made her brave, guided her on as her touch became firmer, her lips dusting its length as he gasped beneath her.

'Make love to me, Clara,' he urged softly.

He knew this was hard for her, knew it was uncharted territory, and as she slowly climbed over and lowered herself onto him he registered the nervousness in her eyes, could almost feel the endearing embarrassed blush as she stared down at him, bracing herself for rejection yet knowing she was wanted.

'Clara, you're beautiful.'

And on any other day, at any other moment, she would have brushed aside his compliment, flicked it away with a scornful response, but seeing the adoration that blazed in his eyes, feeling the reverent way he held her, she accepted it with the grace and confidence of a woman in love, believing, almost, that maybe she was all the wonderful things he whispered.

Leaning forward, she heard his moan of approval as he buried his face in her splendid bosom holding her soft bottom, moving her, guiding her as she rocked above him, bringing them both to the sweet release they so badly needed. Sex for sex's sake perhaps, a primal need that had to be fulfilled, an escape from the reality of the harsh day they had shared, but it was so loaded with love and caring it could never have been called gratuitous.

'Clara?' She heard the question in his voice as they lay spent and entwined, gazing into the darkness, the hazy hormonal rush of their orgasm working its balmy magic. 'What I said today—about Kell, I mean…'

'Don't.' Squeezing her eyes closed, she rushed to stop him. She simply couldn't go there now, couldn't spoil this post-coital peace by revealing the depth of her need for the man that lay beside her, sure it wasn't what he needed to hear tonight of all nights.

'It still hurts, then?' Timothy said softly, kissing her shoulder and pulling her back close as a salty tear slid down her cheek.

Oh, it hurt all right, Clara thought as Timothy's breathing evened out, as the arm that held her tightly gently loosened its grip.

Only her pain had nothing to do with Kell.

CHAPTER NINE

'THESE will be great.' Smiling, Shelly peered over Clara's shoulder at the pile of photographs that lay scattered over the table. 'Abby's going to be thrilled.'

'It's a good idea,' Clara commented, trying to choose between a picture of Kell on a bike and one of Kell on a horse and finally choosing both. 'I mean, I know it's only going to be a tiny wedding, but Kell and his family will be thrilled when they see all of these. If they can't have the wedding in Tennengarrah then why not bring a bit of Tennengarrah to the city?'

'You haven't said anything?' Shelly checked. 'To his dad, I mean. This picture board is supposed to be a surprise.'

'I haven't said a word,' Clara assured her.

'Kell!' Matthew's excited squeak as he grabbed a photo had them both smiling as Clara retrieved it from his jammy fingers.

'It certainly is.' Ruffling his hair, she held it up for all to see. 'Look at this one—we have to include it.'

Both women laughed as they stared at the photo— Kell Bevan at twenty-one years of age, not quite fresh-faced but awkward in his new nursing uniform, standing proudly outside the clinic. But even though she laughed, even though it was fun wading through old photos in such a good cause, Clara's lack of emotion surprised even herself.

Oh, she missed Kell, missed their chats, missed

having another nurse to share the load, missed him as a friend—but that was it.

She didn't love him.

'What are you doing tonight?' Shelly broke into her thoughts and Clara gave a small shrug, trying to keep her voice light.

'Meeting Timothy at the pub.'

'Any special reason?'

Clara looked up, a wry smile on the edge of her lips. 'You tell me, Shelly. Surely Ross must have said something.'

But Shelly shook her head. 'He honestly hasn't, Clara. I know as much as you—he's going to speak to him about it this afternoon when Timothy's finished the clinic.'

'That's honestly all you know?'

Shelly nodded. 'It's my fault. I can't blame Ross. I've told him too many times over the last couple of weeks that I don't want to hear about all the dramas over the staff at the clinic, and now that I actually want to hear the gossip he's torturing me by keeping quiet.'

Clara believed her. Over the last couple of weeks they'd grown closer. Clara had known that even though Matthew was safe now, there would still be some emotional baggage for Shelly to deal with and she had taken it upon herself to be there for her—to ring Shelly and tell her to come over for a coffee and a chat with the kids—and the effort had been worth it tenfold. Finally Clara understood just what Shelly was up against, and in turn Shelly seemed to understand just how much Clara had done for the clinic, how hard it must have been to have relative strangers burst into town and seemingly take things over, and finally a true friendship had been forged…

'So there are two new doctors starting?' Clara checked. 'And possibly a couple more nurses?'

'All I know…' Shelly blew her red curls skyward, searching her mind for a snippet she mightn't have shared '…is that the two doctors are a married couple. He's an anaesthetist, she's a GP, and they're semi-retiring.'

'Has Ross told them there's no such thing as semi-retirement here?' Clara grinned.

'Don't be stupid.' Shelly laughed. 'And scare them off altogether? As for the nurses, they're coming from the agency. I hope they're a bit keener than the one they've already sent. Ross is tearing his hair out!'

'I don't care.' Clara gave a cheeky grin. 'This is my first afternoon off in months and I refuse to feel guilty. Still, it's good that we're finally getting some staff.'

Shelly nodded. 'Ross read the Riot Act and said that until there's more nursing staff we're only going run a skeleton clinic, and finally they seem to have taken notice. But, honestly, Clara, he hasn't said a word about whether he'll be asking Timothy to stay on. Haven't you two spoken about it?'

'There didn't seem much point,' Clara admitted. 'Until we know if there's actually a job for him, it seemed silly to discuss it.'

'Even with two more doctors, there will still be heaps of work,' Shelly said assuredly, but Clara just shook her head.

'I don't doubt that, but what about the budget? Still…' Smiling brightly, Clara stood up, grabbing her bag from the sofa and swinging it over her shoulder.

'With these extra nurses I could take some annual leave. I must have about two years owing by now. Come on, let's head over to the pub.'

'You could join Timothy on his blessed diving course.' Shelly laughed, scooping Kate into her stroller and following her out.

Clara smiled quietly to herself as she walked along, holding Matthew's hand and her breath at the same time.

She'd been thinking exactly the same thing.

One look at Timothy's face and Clara knew it was over.

Knew that the dreams she'd tentatively built in the sand were crashing back into the sea. But she managed a smile, a brave face as Shelly made herself scarce and Timothy came back from the bar, two orange juices in hand and a look she couldn't read on his face.

'I thought you were never coming.' Taking a sip of her drink, she concentrated on keeping her voice light, ignoring her impulse to pick up her bag and run back to her house, to somehow avoid this horrible grown-up conversation that she knew was heading her way.

'You know what Ross can be like when he gets talking.' Timothy shrugged, forcing his own smile but utterly unable to meet her eyes.

'Did he offer to extend your contract?' Her question was brave, the antithesis of how she felt, but the suspense was killing her.

'He did.' For a while he didn't elaborate, just picked up his beer mat between his index finger and thumb and tapped it on the table a few times before setting it down and carefully placing his drink on it. Clara watched—not because it was interesting but, hell, any distraction was welcome, anything was better than having her heart ripped out of her chest without an anaesthetic. 'I'm leaving, Clara.'

Still he didn't look at her—not that Clara was complaining. The chair seemed to be sliding away from beneath her, the world shifting out of focus for a second or two as she struggled to take the finality of his words in. She waited with a growing sense of futility for Timothy to elaborate, to shyly smile and ask her to come on his travels with him, but he didn't. Instead, he picked up his drink and the blessed beer mat as the pub carried on around them, as the world kept right on turning even though for Clara it might just as well stop now.

'I'm not what Tennengarrah needs,' he said in low, subdued tones. 'They've got two new doctors starting—one's an anaesthetist, for heaven's sake. If Ross is serious about upgrading the clinic then surely the most sensible thing would be to employ a surgeon, not blow a shaky budget on a very junior doctor.'

'Where's he going to find a surgeon?' Clara pointed out. 'It's taken months to get this far. Surely you can stay until he finds someone.'

'Ross said the same.'

'Then why don't you?'

Finally he looked at her, those beautiful green eyes unusually guarded, that beautiful open face so lined with tension it was as if she were looking at a stranger, the harshness in his voice alien to her ears.

'I don't want to be a fill in, Clara. I don't want to be second best. Call me conceited, call me what you will, but I happen to think I deserve better than that.

If I'm staying here it has to because I'm needed, because it's me and me alone that's wanted, and a junior doctor just isn't on the top of the wish list here. I've worked hard to get my medical degree. I know I'm not the best doctor in the world but I am a good doctor and I need to do more training, need to get back out there and be all I know I can be...' His wrist caught her hand, forcing her attention, forcing her to look back at him. 'Can you understand that?'

She could.

Oh, she didn't have to like it, but put like that she could understand it, and there and then she berated herself for her optimism, for her stupid wasted dreams of a future beside Timothy. Why would someone with his knowledge, with his passion end his career before it had even begun? Why would someone as beautiful and as wondrous as Timothy throw it all in for someone like her?

'When will you go?'

'I've already packed up the ute.' Aghast, she whipped her face up to him, but he just shook his head. 'I can't settle for being second best, Clara.'

'Then don't.' She registered his frown, knew that she had confused him, and she used the brief pause to clear her throat, to somehow fashion a response. And because she loved him, because this was how they'd both agreed it would end, because she'd do anything to make things easier for him, she did the hardest, bravest thing she'd ever done in her life. 'You're right to move on. Of course I'd love you to stay longer, we both know that. But as good as it's been, we both knew it was never going to be for ever.'

'What about you?' Timothy said gently. 'Will you be all right?'

'I'll be just fine.' Clara swallowed hard, even managed a semblance of a smile. 'I promise not to get drunk and try to declare undying love to you outside the barn. But I will miss you, Timothy.'

She watched as he stood up, drained his drink and offered her his arm. 'I know. Come on, let's get out of here.'

'You go.' Her voice was curiously high. 'We both know I'm lousy at goodbyes.'

'So that's it?' Timothy rasped, but Clara refused to be drawn. 'That's all we're worth. What? Am I supposed to shake your hand or something? Do you want me to say I'll send a postcard?'

'You're the one leaving, Timothy,' Clara pointed out, sarcasm uncharacteristically dripping off her tongue as she continued. 'If you'd given me a bit more notice, I could maybe have rustled up something a bit grander, a cake perhaps or a—'

'Don't.' He closed his eyes but not quickly enough to hide the pain there. Clara finally relented, holding onto his hand as he quietly said goodbye to Ross and a teary Shelly, holding it together as they walked hand in hand towards his dusty and not particularly trusty ute with a heart that didn't feel as if it was beating any more. She closed her eyes for a final goodbye kiss, staring for an age as his ute pulled off into the darkness and stared at the rear lights disappearing along with her soul mate.

Wandering back into the house, she didn't even cry, didn't throw herself on the bed or break down in hysterics—just stared at her house, empty now without Timothy's clutter, his boots gone from the hall, the ton of mess he so effortlessly generated.

Sitting down at the table, she buried her face in her

hands. Kell's images stared back at her and she gazed unseeingly at the photographs, scarcely able to believe that she'd thought she'd loved him.

Hardly able to believe the pain she had thought she had felt when Kell had left, because nothing compared to the loss she felt now, nothing at all.

It was as if she had lost her soul.

CHAPTER TEN

LIFE for Clara continued on autopilot.

A numb state of shock as the days dragged on end-lessly and the nights seemed to last for ever.

Even her once busy schedule dwindled with the arrival of fresh faces, so she didn't even have the saving grace of burying herself in her work.

Time was on her hands when she needed it least.

Dressing listlessly one morning, she stared at her empty bed, missing that smiling face on the pillow, sighing wearily as a button flew off her blouse. Since Timothy had left, routine had gone to pot. The mess he generated had been replaced by Clara's now. Normally meticulous, her ironing basket groaned un-der its own weight, every last work blouse a crumpled mess that would take for ever to iron. She located a needle but finding the thread took a bit longer, hell, even stitching on a button these days required a mas-sive effort of concentration. But finally the job was done and Clara slipped on her blouse, grimacing when she saw the clock and realised that for the first time in her nursing career she was going to be late.

Only when the second button rolled onto the floor did the penny start to drop.

OK, being a seamstress wasn't up there on her list of talents but even *she* knew how to sew on a button. Looking down at her blouse, Clara knew there and then that nothing short of metal wiring was going to hold her blouse together. Her breasts, always large, seemed to have taken on a life of their own.

Fingering her waistband, Clara knew she wasn't imagining things. She'd been the same size for ever, now all of a sudden those smart navy culottes were definitely tight on her.

Definitely.

Under any other circumstances the knowledge would have sent her into a spin, but nothing seemed to matter any more. Since Timothy had gone she'd felt as if she were on beta-blockers, as if she were taking a cardiac drug that permanently steadied her heart rate, kept her blood pressure even.

Nothing seemed to matter.

Slipping off her skirt, she lay back on the bed, moving her hands down her soft white stomach, fingers gently probing until...

Clara had felt more stomachs than she could count, knew what a fundus felt like, the soft regular shape of the tip of the uterus as it bobbed out of the pelvic brim, a tiny life pushing the womb upwards as it grew inside. Suddenly the metaphorical beta-blockers must have worn off, because her heart rate was picking up, her blood pressure crashing through the roof as her body spoke for itself.

Rolling onto her side, she clung onto the pillow for comfort, closing her eyes in an attempt to block out the obvious truth.

'Oh, no,' she whispered, her hands moving down to her stomach again. 'What have I done?'

'Sixteen weeks.' Ross didn't look over, just stared at the screen as he clicked away taking measurements, his voice matter-of-fact, ever the professional, but Clara could hear the kindness behind it.

'I can't be, Ross.' Clara shook her head against the white-papered pillow. 'I've had periods.'

'When?'

Her eyebrows furrowed as she forced her mind to think. 'I've never been particularly regular but I know I've had them...' Her eyes opened wide. 'I had one last month, just after Timothy left. I can remember thinking, Great, that's all I need now. So you see...'

'It wasn't a period,' Ross said gently. 'Some women get bleeding in the first trimester when their periods would have been due...'

'But I'm on the Pill.' She knew her argument was futile, that the image staring back at her from the screen was irrefutable evidence if ever she'd needed it, but still she begged, stabbed at the chance to change the inevitable. 'I take it every morning. I've never missed, Ross, not even once.'

'You had gastro a while back,' Ross reminded her gently, 'when Timothy first started. I remember because Shelly had to fill in for you.'

'But we were careful.'

'Sometimes the damage is already done,' Ross said gently. 'Maybe the Pill you took before you got sick wasn't properly absorbed and if the timing was right, if you'd just ovulated and...' His voice trailed off. 'I'm sure you don't need a biology lesson, Clara. These things just happen sometimes.'

'But sixteen weeks,' Clara begged. 'How could I not have known?'

'It's too small for you to feel it move yet, and I guess with Timothy gone you've had your mind on other things.'

Ross was right on that count, but at just the mention of his name Clara felt her eyes fill up, the true horror of her situation starting to dawn.

'He's a nice guy,' Ross said softly. 'I'm sure he'll stand by you.'

'I don't want him to stand by me,' Clara sniffed, accepting the tissue Ross offered.

'It's going to be long, lonely pregnancy without him,' Ross pushed. 'Even taking into account the sixteen weeks you've managed to get through unwittingly. He'd want to be there.'

But Clara shook her head. 'To hold my hands during antenatal classes?' She gave a low laugh. 'I'm the one who gives the classes, Ross. I know what pregnancy involves, I know what I'm up against...'

'For the next few months perhaps,' Ross's voice remained even. 'But once that baby comes along, everything changes, Clara. It doesn't matter what your qualifications are, how well you think you're prepared. At the end of the day a baby will turn your world around.' He gave a wry smile. 'If Timothy were here, he'd tell me off now for assuming that just because I've got children I think I know it all.'

Clara gave a puzzled frown as Ross continued.

'He read me the Riot Act his first week here when I insisted that you take care of Eileen. He'd stand by you, Clara.'

'Exactly.' She blinked. 'And the very last thing I'll need is a reluctant partner.'

'He has to be told.'

'No, he doesn't,' Clara responded fiercely. 'Lots of women bring up children on their own these days. There's lots of single mums. Shelly managed on her own.'

'Shelly managed,' Ross said gently, 'but *managed* just about sums it up. There was no time to enjoy motherhood, no one to share Matthew's milestones with—just endless responsibility and angst. Shelly will tell you the same herself. It would be so much easier for you to share this with someone.'

'Not if he doesn't love me,' Clara responded. 'I know he's a nice guy, so nice that no doubt he'll do the right thing, give up all of his dreams of being a surgeon and come back and support me, but I can't live like that, Ross. Timothy said on the day he left that he didn't want to settle for second best and, frankly, neither do I. If he didn't love me enough to stay, I don't want to force him to come back.'

'I'm sorry, Clara,' Ross sighed. 'I really tried to change his mind. When I first offered him the job I thought he was going to take it. He raced back to the house, said he was going to talk things over with you. I had a bottle of champagne ready, I really thought he was staying, then suddenly he changed his mind. Said the outback wasn't for him.'

'That's not what Timothy said.' Clara frowned. 'He made it sound as if you didn't really want him, as if you were just offering him a job because you felt you had to.'

'Clara!' Ross's eyes were wide. 'I'd have given anything to keep Timothy here. He's going to be a great doctor. I even explained that once the clinic moved up a stage and we had a few more doctors on board, he could do a formal rotation here or we'd second him to go the city and get some more courses under his belt. I'd have given anything to keep him.'

'So would I,' Clara managed, turning her face to the wall, eternally grateful when Ross flicked off the machine and pulled the curtain quietly around her, leaving her alone with her thoughts and a little black-and-white photo of the life inside her which she stared at for an age.

'So would I,' she sobbed.

CHAPTER ELEVEN

'YOU'RE supposed to be putting on weight,' Shelly admonished gently as Clara stepped off the scales. 'Not losing it.'

Clara gave a tired shrug. 'And you're supposed to be at home with your children, Shelly. I feel awful dragging you out. One of the others could have seen me.'

'Oh, come on, Clara, you're my one and only patient, I'm hardly slaving away. Anyway, I wouldn't miss this for the world.' When Clara didn't smile back Shelly steered her to the small examination couch. 'Ross wants to come and talk to you, Clara.'

'Is something wrong?'

'He's concerned that you're doing too much and, frankly, so am I. You're twenty-eight weeks now, it's time to be cutting down your workload.'

'I've cut right back,' Clara argued. 'I only see a handful of patients now.'

'All the difficult ones,' Shelly pointed out. 'Look, Clara, the baby's a nice size, all your obs are fine, your urine's as clear as a bell, but it doesn't take a nursing degree to know that a pregnant woman's weight is supposed to go upwards. You haven't put an ounce on for four weeks now. You have to learn to delegate a bit more, let the new staff take over some of the load. In a few short weeks you're going to be on maternity leave and, as much as you don't believe me now, this little one is going to take up every last piece of what's left of your brain.'

'I can't stop seeing Eileen now,' Clara moaned. 'She's just finished her last round of chemo and you know how rough it's been for her. She's got an MRI next week and she's terrified.'

'Then go and see her with a cake instead of your nurse's bag. Just because you're not working, it doesn't mean you can't be her friend.'

But Clara shook her head. 'I promised I'd be there for her. I'm heading over there after here.' Seeing Shelly frown, Clara got in first. 'OK, I'll talk to her,' she sighed. 'Maybe Jenny could take over, she seems really nice.'

'She *is* really nice,' Shelly said firmly. 'Anyway, with a bit of luck Eileen will get the all-clear and then you really won't have an excuse not to put your feet up.

'You still haven't heard from Timothy, I take it?'

'Nothing,' Clara sighed. She slipped up her top and Shelly gently probed her abdomen.

'It's only been a couple of weeks since you wrote and it's not as if you've got an address. If Timothy's having his mail redirected, it could take ages for him to get the letter.'

'Has Ross had any luck?' Clara asked hopefully, but Shelly shook her head.

'We've only got his parents' address and phone number in England. Maybe you should ring them. We've tried every diving school in the phone book and got nowhere. Perhaps he headed home after all.'

'Perhaps.' Clara shrugged, swallowing back the familiar lump in her throat as Shelly pulled down the maternity top then perched herself on the couch beside her. 'But from the little Timothy told me, he's not exactly on great terms with his parents. I don't want to make things more awkward for him and I'm sure a pregnant ex-girlfriend isn't the kind of holiday memento he was hoping to collect. I'd rather try and find him myself before I resort to getting his parents involved.'

'Ross could ring them.' Shelly grinned. 'Say we've underpaid him, that there's this huge cheque here with his name on it—that should get a result.' When that didn't even raise a smile Shelly's voice softened as she pushed a touch further. 'How come you changed your mind, Clara? You were so adamant you didn't want him involved before.'

'I'd love him to be involved,' Clara corrected, 'but only if that was what he really wanted.' Taking a deep breath, she stared down at the mound of her abdomen and ran a hand over it. 'I was lying in the bath and suddenly the baby moved. Not just a little bit, mind, my whole stomach seemed to flip over...'

'Amazing, isn't it?'

Clara nodded. 'I just lay there watching it, and for the first time I actually realised there was a person in there, not just a baby, not just my bump, but a person. And I figured Timothy deserved to know about it.'

'He does,' Shelly said softly. 'You know Ross isn't Matthew's real father?' She gave a soft laugh. 'Or rather you know that Ross isn't Matthew's biological father?'

Clara nodded.

'Neil, my ex-husband, didn't want to know about Matthew, figured a special needs child was just too dammed hard for the life he'd lined up. Now Matthew will never know any different, he adores Ross and that's enough for him.' Her hands moved to Clara's bump, resting her hands there softly for a moment. 'God willing, this little one won't have any of Matthew's problems. God willing, this little person will grow up to be a nosy, inquisitive, intelligent child and you're going to have to answer some difficult questions. Imagine how hard it would be to look this *person* in the eye and say you didn't even tell their father they existed. It's easy to make choices now but eventually you'll have to face them.'

'I know,' Clara gulped. 'And if I don't hear from him in the next week I'll ring his family.' Accepting Shelly's hand, she hauled herself of the couch, blowing her nose loudly on a tissue before turning to face her friend.

'Thanks, Shelly.'

'I haven't finished yet. Our house at six. Roast and veggies and extra-thick gravy.'

'It's forty degrees outside,' Clara moaned.

'I don't care. You need some calories. I might even make a chocolate cake if you're lucky.'

'With custard?' Clara checked, her glittering, tear-filled eyes all the thanks Shelly needed.

'*Chocolate* custard.' Shelly smiled. 'And if I have a glass of wine I might even ring Timothy's parents myself!'

Pulling the Jeep to a halt outside Eileen's, Clara reached over to the passenger seat for her bag, her mind totally focused on the meeting ahead, mentally preparing herself, the sight of Eileen's bald head, her painfully thin, emaciated body still a shock after all this time.

The strength of the contraction that gripped her was another shock.

Breathing out through her mouth, leaning back on the driver's seat, Clara waited for it to pass, her hands instinctively moving to her stomach, feeling the firm mass of her uterus tight against her palms, her eyes flicking to the dashboard clock, counting the seconds then breathing a sigh of relief when it ended.

Braxton-Hicks' contractions.

With a rueful laugh she scooped up her bag and climbed out of the Jeep, the hot midday sun scorching the back of her neck as she walked towards Eileen's home. How many first-time mums had rung her, terrified they were about to go into labour, sure that the irregular false contractions they were experiencing were the real thing?

'When you're toes are curling it's the real thing,' Clara had always said, popping them on to the CTG monitor to prove beyond doubt that all they'd been feeling had been mother nature's warm-up run. Even as she walked she closed her eyes for a second. One day in the not too distant future her toes *would* be curling, her baby—*their* baby—would be coming into the world, and not for the first time Clara felt a wave of panic at the inevitability of it all. The journey she had unwittingly embarked on, one that until now she had chosen to travel alone. But as the weeks had passed into months, reality had started to hit, and now more than ever she needed Timothy beside her, needed him with her.

Missed him so much.

'Only me.'

The days of knocking and politely waiting on the doorstep had long since gone. Instead, Clara pushed open the fly screen as she called out and made her way straight through to the living room, smiling at her friend who lay supported by a mountain of pillows on the sofa, a brightly coloured scarf wrapped around her head, a splash of lipstick out of place on her thin, pale face, but Clara was thrilled to see it all the same. Thrilled that Eileen was making an effort, taking a pride in her appearance.

Still hanging in there.

'I've done my fingernails.' Eileen smiled, replacing the lid on her bottle of nail varnish and holding up her hand as Clara admired her handiwork. 'But I haven't the energy to do my toenails.'

'I know the feeling,' Clara groaned, 'though in my case I can barely reach them. I can do them for you.' Settling herself down, she undid the lid and set to work, glad for the small distraction, the chance to talk without her words sounding horribly rehearsed. 'So, how are you doing?'

'What version do you want to hear?' Eileen sighed.

'The truth will do,' Clara said, without looking up. 'Are you scared about next week?'

'Terrified,' Eileen admitted. 'Last night I took one of those sleeping tablets that Timothy prescribed me. I hadn't taken even one before, the bottle's just been sitting there in the medicine cupboard along with the hundred others.'

'That's what they were prescribed for,' Clara responded matter-of-factly, but even the mention of Timothy's name had a tiny blush dusting her cheeks. 'It's important that you get your rest after all you've been through.'

'I know,' Eileen sighed. 'I just wish it was this time

next week, wish I knew if all this treatment had worked.' She gave a low laugh. 'Then again maybe I don't.'

With ten toes painted Clara finally looked up. 'Let's just wait and see, shall we? Whatever the results, we'll cross that bridge when we come to it. Focus on the positives.'

'What positives?'

'Heidi's at school,' Clara said gently, 'and, as hellish as the treatments been, you've had six more months.'

'I want more.' Eileen's voice was hoarse and her request was so basic, so much her entitlement, Clara simply didn't know what to say.

'I'd better do your bloods,' she said instead, reaching down to her bag. 'The results will come to Ross, but they'll also go to your oncologist in Adelaide in time for your appointment next—'

'Are you all right, Clara?'

She didn't answer straight away. Bent over her bag, she stilled for a moment, and then looked up, smiling assuredly. 'Next time an anxious mum rings me about Braxton-Hicks' contractions I won't be so blasé. They're actually quite strong, *aren't they*?'

Eileen gave a small frown. The question in Clara's voice hadn't gone unnoticed. The slight shift in tone told her that Clara was asking for reassurance, but Eileen wasn't sure she could give it. 'They can be strong,' Eileen started slowly, 'but I don't think they should stop you talking!' She gave a nervous laugh. 'Mind you, it could just be me. Nothing ever stopped me talking, not even childbirth. I was roaring at Jerry the whole way through. Even after two rounds of chemo I was still cursing loudly, albeit with my head down the toilet...' Her voice trailed off as Clara sat back in the sofa, her hand moving protectively to her bump, her eyes closing as another spasm gripped her. 'Do you want me to ring Ross?'

Eileen waited, waited for Clara to look up, to smile reassuringly and say 'Don't be daft', but when her troubled blue eyes finally opened, when Clara gave a small, nervous nod, her stiff upper lip actually trembling, Eileen pulled herself up.

'Tell him to come straight away.' Her voice was trembling as she spoke. 'Tell him to bring Shelly and the emergency delivery pack. Tell them to ring the Flying—'

'They'll know what to do,' Eileen said bravely. 'You just stay there and try to stay calm.' She patted Clara's shoulders, ignoring her aching body's protests she raced into the hall, returning moments later and joining Clara on the sofa, where she put her arms around her. And suddenly it wasn't a nurse and patient any more, it wasn't even about two friends.

Just two scared women, staring out of the window as they held each other.

Two women, quite simply praying for time.

CHAPTER TWELVE

'THREE centimetres dilated.' Ross fixed Clara with a reassuring smile as Shelly pulled the duvet back around her. 'That's good.'

'No, it isn't,' Clara sobbed. 'It's way too soon...'

'Three centimetres,' Ross carried on over her, 'and your membranes are intact and the contractions seem to be easing off a bit by themselves. We might be able to stop the labour at this stage. Even if we can delay it for twelve hours, that will mean the steroids I'll give you will have time to take effect, they'll help to mature the baby's lungs, but with a bit of luck we'll be able to stop the labour altogether. Now, I'm going to radio through this information and see what the Flying Doctors say. They should be here soon, but it's probably better that we get these drugs started.' He gave a thin smile and Clara knew what was coming.

'You'll need an IV and a catheter.'

'I'll do it.' Shelly shooed him out. 'You get on the radio.'

'Thanks for both of you coming,' Clara said when they were alone. 'Are the kids outside with Eileen?'

'They're back at the house,' Shelly said lightly— too lightly, Clara realised. 'June's watching them for me.'

Lying back on the pillow, Clara knew then that she was loved.

Neither Matthew nor Kate had been more than two

feet away from Shelly since Matthew's disappearing act, and the fact she had jumped into the Jeep and raced to get here for her told Clara the true depth of their friendship.

Shelly was very gentle as she inserted the catheter, talking away to take away the sting of embarrassment, and also very professional, but Clara could see the sparkle of tears in her eyes as she flushed the IV.

'This isn't your fault, Shelly,' Clara said gently. 'You know as well as I do that these things happen sometimes. I was fine earlier, not even a twinge, there was nothing to suggest—'

'I know,' Shelly sniffed, 'but two can play at that game, so if it isn't my fault it most certainly isn't yours. I don't want you beating yourself up, wondering if there was something you could have done to prevent this.'

'I'll try,' Clara sighed. 'You've no idea how many women I've said the same thing to, but it's not so easy to be objective when it's your own baby.

'Shelly.'

Something in Clara's voice made Shelly look up.

'Ross told me Timothy had a go at you both once, that he said just because someone doesn't have children it didn't mean they didn't get upset.'

Shelly nodded. 'He was right to say something. I used to get annoyed about the same thing when I worked on the children's ward before Matthew came along. Other nurses would bang on, saying I didn't know how the parents felt because I'd never had my own. It was the same when I did my midwifery, as if I couldn't possibly know what I was talking about because I'd never had a baby.

'I was being selfish,' Shelly finished.

'You were being truthful,' Clara said softly. 'I've never been more scared in my life, never really knew what it was all about until now. I love this baby and I can understand where you were coming from. Timothy shouldn't have said anything.'

Shelly said simply, 'He was just sticking up for you.'

But there was no time for introspection because suddenly the room was filled with personnel and equipment. Dr Hall strolled in, managing to roll his eyes and wink at the same time as he saw Clara lying pale and terrified on the bed.

'My wife's going to love you,' he joked. 'She's after a new kitchen and this one will push me into overtime.' His voice softened as he parked his huge frame on the bed beside her, one rough yet tender hand gently on her stomach as he quietly studied his watch. 'The old way's the best way.' He looked up and held her terrified eyes. 'The medication we're giving you will hopefully slow things down. Now, Ross has already examined you and taken swabs so I'm not going to disturb things while they're quiet as, no doubt, they'll want to check you again at the hospital.'

Clara nodded. Hall's explanations were kept simple and she was grateful, her mind not really up to lengthy explanations. And though she knew all the answers, though she'd been through the scenario before, now she was at the receiving end all her training seemed to have flown out of the window. 'What if I deliver on the way, Hall? Twenty-eight weeks is just too early.'

'We've seen smaller, though, haven't we, Clara?' Pulling her top back down, he gave her a reassuring smile. 'If you do deliver then we've got everything on the plane, but I reckon this little tacker's going to stay put at least till we get to Adelaide, for what it's worth.'

Oh, it was worth so much.

Hall's quiet words of encouragement were everything she needed right now.

Clara managed a brave smile as he stood up, gave the signal to get things moving, until finally, with tubes coming out everywhere, machines strapped to most of her body, she knew it was time to go.

'I'm going with her.' Shelly's voice was firm, but Clara heard the emotion behind it.

'Shelly, I'll be fine,' Clara said quickly, but Shelly was resolute.

'You're not facing this on your own.' Her voice trembled slightly as she took Clara's hand. 'Ross can take a couple of days off and watch the children. You're not going to Adelaide without someone beside you.'

'Do you want to have that word with Clara, Ross?' Hall's words didn't make sense and both Shelly and Clara looked up in surprise as Ross gave a small tentative nod.

'Two minutes,' Hall said to Ross, and then smiled down at his patient. 'I'll just make sure the plane's ready.'

Clara knew the plane was ready, knew he was just being polite, but as she turned her inquisitive eyes to Ross, her curiosity turned to nervousness as he asked Shelly to wait outside.

'What is it, Ross?' she ventured when they were finally alone. 'What's happened? Is it the baby?'

'The baby's fine.' Ross was quick to reassure her.

'For the moment anyway. The contractions are slowing down now. It's not the baby I need to talk to you about.'

'Then what?' She'd never seen Ross so lost for words and his evasiveness scared her. 'Come on, Ross, tell me.'

'Clara, you know you have to stay calm—you know that, don't you?' he checked as she nodded, bewildered. 'I really didn't want to tell you now, but I don't think I have a choice. I've discussed it with Hall—'

'You're scaring me, Ross,' Clara broke in.

'I'm sorry.' Taking her hands, he looked her straight in the eye. 'Timothy rang this morning.' When Clara didn't respond he carried on gently, 'He didn't say much. He'd tried to phone you at home, and then he rang the clinic. When I said you were out on a visit he said he'd ring back tonight.'

'Has he got my letter?'

Ross gave a small shrug. 'I don't think so, Clara. Like I said, he didn't say much, but my take on it was that he just missed you, that he wanted to talk to you.'

'Did you tell him?' Clara asked, her eyes filling up. 'About the baby, I mean? I promise I won't be cross. In some ways I hope you have…'

'I didn't tell him,' Ross said slowly. 'I didn't know then there was a problem, but even if he rings now, unless you want me to tell him I still can't. Do you understand that?'

She nodded, and as the news sank in so the questions started. 'Is he doing his diving course?'

Ross shook his head.

'He's moved back to England, then?'

She sensed his hesitancy, and she moved to reassure him. 'You can tell me, Ross, I've prepared myself for it.'

Oh, no, she hadn't. As Ross looked up, as his hands tightened around hers, as he started to speak, she finally understood his nervousness, why he had begged her to stay calm.

'Timothy's in Adelaide,' he said slowly, and Clara's eyes widened, the air catching in her throat as she struggled to take a deep breath, to force herself to stay calm as her handle on the world jolted into overdrive. 'He's doing a rotation at the hospital you're going to, Clara. Do you see now why I had to tell you?'

She didn't answer, just lay back on the hard stretcher as the news sank in, the next contraction barely meriting a comment. Ross's words had been like a hand grenade thrown into her brain, scrambling everything, blowing every preconceived idea she'd had about how to tell Timothy, the impact of his words ricocheting through every cell in her body. But as the shock abated, as reality filtered back in, far from desolation, far from the cold fingers of fear that had gripped as her labour had taken hold, Clara was left with a curious sense of calm, a small sense that all was right.

In a couple of hours or so she would see Timothy again.

'Do you want me to ring the hospital?' Ross broke into the smoldering aftermath that used to be her brain, concern etched on every feature as he awaited her reaction. 'I can tell him, if that's what you want. It might give him some time to get his head around the idea before you arrive.'

Clara thought for a moment before answering. Under any other circumstances she would have told him herself, his reaction to the news something she wanted—no, needed—to witness. But there was the baby to think of, a baby too small for this world, and emotional confrontations had to be avoided at all costs.

'Tell him I'm sorry,' Clara said softly. 'Tell him that I never wanted him to find out like this.'

'Of course.' As Hall tapped softly at the door Ross stood up. 'I had to tell Hall. I couldn't really just jump in and tell you without him being aware of what was going on, and we all know how nosy Timothy is. A chopper landing is just the sort of thing that would fuel his curiosity. I didn't fancy him wandering in for a sticky beak, only to see you lying on the stretcher. But apart from that, it's between you and I.'

'You can tell Shelly.' Clara smiled, noting the relieved look that washed over his face. 'I know she'd make your life hell otherwise.'

Ross smiled. 'She and Eileen probably have her stethoscope to the wall as we speak. I'm only kidding. Shelly would never—'

'I know.'

'You're taking this very well,' Ross murmured, as Hall made his presence known again. 'If you want Shelly to come with you, the offer's there.'

'I'll be fine.' Clara smiled as the stretcher moved down the hallway, her hand wrapped around her stomach. 'I mean *we'll* be fine.'

'One out, two in,' Eileen said tearfully as they carefully lifted the stretcher down the front steps. 'Warn the hospital to expect lots of calls!'

*   *   *

Clara didn't remember much about the flight, just lay back and tried to stay calm, to focus on the tiny life within in her and not be too greedy with her prayers.

Twelve more weeks would be pushing it, Clara admitted as she listened to the blips on the monitor beside her. She'd even settle for twelve more days, knowing every day *in utero* was the best chance her baby had.

Twelve hours even…

'Another one?' Hall's hand was back on her stomach, his other one reaching for Clara's as she willed the contraction to end, willed the pain to subside. But it seemed to go on for ever and she gripped Hall's hand harder, moaning in terror as she felt her own toes curl now, knew however much she didn't want to admit it that things were starting to move.

'My back hurts,' she sobbed, retching into a bowl the nurse quickly held out as the activity on the plane started to lift, the anaesthetist pulling up drugs, the nurse calmly opening packs. But her nonchalance didn't fool Clara for a minute.

'How long till we get there, Hall?'

'Another fifteen minutes or so, but if we don't make it, it doesn't matter. We've got everything we need here, Clara.' His words didn't comfort her and she shook her head, her eyes imploring him to stop, to listen and to act.

'I have to get there,' she sobbed, doubling over as another contraction engulfed her, the straps of the stretcher biting into her legs as she sought some comfort, desperate to kneel up, to rock back on her heels, to give in to her body and let the baby come. But still she fought it, willing herself to stay calm, breathing though the pain till it blissfully subsided. 'I have to get to Adelaide, Hall.' He gave a tight nod, pushing drugs through the IV line as the nurse slipped an oxygen mask over her face.

'We're doing everything we can, Clara.' He was fiddling with the IV pump as the anaesthetist passed him another spring. 'Just try and relax, give the medication a chance to work…'

She did as she was told, lying back on the pillow, listening to the pilot radioing through her progress, imagining the scene at the other end, the nurses and doctors waiting, the delivery ward being set up. And Timothy confused and bewildered, the news still sinking in, racing out to the landing strip as the efficient staff waited for the landing. Imagining how hard it must be for him to make sense of it all, trying to tell the waiting crowd that this was *his* child they were expecting…

It didn't look like Timothy.

As the stretcher was moved swiftly from the plane she scanned the faces, Timothy's the only one that mattered now, and as their eyes locked she knew his pain surely equalled hers.

Lines she had never seen before seemed to be grooved into his face. Those smiling eyes were alien now, hurt, bewildered and utterly terrified as he ran along beside the stretcher, unfamiliar in a suit and tie, his white coat flapping behind him as he raced alongside her, squeezing himself into the lift and impatiently turning off his pager, which was bleeping noisily, adding to the fraught confusion that surrounded her.

'I'm sorry,' she started, pulling off the oxygen mask as the lift doors closed, but he shook his head, replacing the mask with shaking hands, his voice gruff and thick with emotion.

'Keep it on,' he said. 'The baby needs it.' His eyes dragged to the portable monitors that surrounded her. 'You need it, too.'

'But—'

'Not now, Clara,' he said firmly. 'We'll talk later.'

And with that she had to make do.

Hall stayed, relaying his treatment to the attending doctors and midwives as they changed over the machines to the delivery ward's own. A cast of thousands seemed to be crammed into the room, separate teams for Clara and the baby, preparing the resuscitation cot and talking in the low urgent voices Clara knew only too well.

'It sounded as if you were having it.' Timothy's voice was a croak.

'When did Ross ring?' She couldn't look at him and it would seem Timothy was having the same problem as his eyes were fixed on the monitor, watching the baby's heart rate and the strength of Clara's contractions.

'An hour or so ago.' He glanced at his watch. 'A bit more maybe. Everyone seemed pretty laid-back, but just as you were due in they radioed through that they were expecting you to deliver *en route*, and the whole place went crazy.'

'It was the same on board.' Clara lay back, closing her eyes as another contraction came, but it was mercifully short and the pain she'd anticipated didn't eventuate.

'I said I'd get you here.' Hall smiled, coming over.

'Thank you so much,' Clara whispered, but Hall just shook his head.

'No. Thank *you*. It makes cleaning up and restocking so much easier,' he said, but the humour didn't quite cover up the emotion in his voice. 'You're in the right place now,' he added softly, 'and the drugs seem to be kicking in a bit. Hopefully this little tacker will stay put a while longer.'

Timothy hovered as the bustle in the room carried on, the drama of an impending birth receding as Clara's contractions died down. And finally, when every last test known had been performed, when surely her haemoglobin must now be in its boots from the amount of blood that had been taken, with wires and monitors coming from everywhere, Casey, the midwife, gave her a slow but optimistic smile.

'Get some sleep,' she suggested. 'I'll put the lights down and let you rest.' She looked over at Timothy, who stood awkwardly at the foot of the bed. 'You, too,' she added, pulling up a chair and gesturing for him to sit. 'You could both be in for a long night— you should try and conserve a bit of energy.'

But sleep would have to wait a while. Left alone in the semi-darkness, they listened to the regular bleeps of the monitors for what seemed like an age until finally Clara broke the strained silence.

'I'm sorry,' she started again. 'It must have been awful to find out this way.'

'Leave it, Clara,' Timothy said in a tight voice. 'Do what the midwife said and get some rest.'

'I can't rest, though,' she responded tearfully. 'I can't just lie back and close my eyes when you're—'

'Do you want me to leave?' Timothy offered. 'If it will make things easier, I can wait outside.'

But Clara shook her head. The thought of him leaving her now brought no peace at all. 'I don't want to fight, but I also know that there's a lot of things that need to be said, and until we at least talk I can't rest. If we can just get it over with—'

'Get it over with?' His voice was incredulous and he struggled to control it. 'Believe me, Clara, this won't be over with in a matter of minutes. Don't lie on the bed like some sort of martyr asking me for absolution, because I can't give it now. That's my baby you're carrying and you let me leave without even telling me it existed.'

'I didn't know,' she said quickly as he gave an unbelieving snort. 'I honestly didn't, not till about a month after you'd left. I thought I was having periods. Remember when I ran out of…?' Her voice trailed off but her words seemed to have reached him and finally he sat down, his face not exactly friendly but, hell, she'd settle for any improvement right now. 'I found out at sixteen weeks.'

'Excuse my maths, Clara, but if I'm not mistaken sixteen from twenty-eight makes twelve. That's twelve weeks you've had to let me know I was about to become a father. If you hadn't come here, if it hadn't been inevitable I'd find out, would I still be in the dark? Was this baby going to grow up not knowing I existed?'

'I wrote.'

'So we're blaming the postman now?' Sarcasm didn't suit him and he changed tack quickly. The delivery ward was no place for a row. 'All I ever did was love you, Clara.'

'You left,' she pointed out, and Timothy raked a shaking hand though his hair. 'It didn't look like love to me.'

'Do you blame me?' His voice was a raw whisper.

'Did you expect me just to live in Kell's shadow? Hell, a second-rate doctor I could just about have swallowed, but a second-rate lover?'

'You were never second rate,' Clara said. 'I was scared to tell you how much you meant to me, scared of being a burden.'

Confused eyes met hers and Timothy stood up slowly. 'We can't do this now, Clara, there's just too much hurt there. I can't go over it all and be expected to stay calm, and neither can you. For now we just have to put it all to one side and get through this any way we can. We've got the baby to think of.

'Our baby,' he added softly, his hand tentatively moving to the ripe mound of her stomach. 'Can I?'

She nodded, watching his face as his hand met her skin, watching his eyes squeeze tightly on tears as a tiny foot or hand made its presence felt, greeting the very new father-to-be with a deft little jab. And as beautiful as the moment was, it was laced for Clara with regret, regret for all Timothy had missed out on.

Casey popped her head around the door, smiling as she came over. 'Hop on if you like,' she suggested, pulling down the side of the bed as Timothy stood there awkwardly. 'If it helps Clara to relax then it's all in a good cause.'

'Will it help?' His eyes searched Clara's face and she nodded slowly, moving over a touch as Timothy climbed on top of the sheet, both awkward and shy as Casey pulled up the side rail.

'We don't want you both toppling out. Reading the monitors, she quietly wrote down Clara's and the baby's obs before turning. 'We'll be in and out all night, but just buzz if you need anything.'

Timothy held her, his movements awkward at first

as Clara lay there, rigid and nervous and wondering if it was such a good idea, but as his hand rested on her bump, as he pulled her in just a little bit tighter, their stage fright vanished, many nights holding each other the best dress rehearsal of all.

'Clara?' She heard the anxiety in his voice as she pulled herself up, the monitors going crazy as the lights flooded on, nurses appearing from everywhere as they pulled down the side of the bed and Timothy jumped off, sleepy and dazed at first but snapping to attention in a matter of seconds.

'I can't breathe,' she gasped, her hand clutching the mask over her face, every breath an effort as her heart seemed to gallop inside her chest.

'It's OK, Clara.' Casey's voice was reassuring above the confusion. 'I've turned up the oxygen. Just take some nice slow deep breaths—the doctor's on his way.'

'What's happening?' Timothy's hand gripped hers tightly as she whispered the words, too tired to look up, too exhausted to do anything other than try and breathe.

'She's having trouble breathing.' Casey's words reached her from a distance and Clara realised she was addressing Timothy.

'I can see that,' Timothy responded, the anxiety clear in his voice. 'What I want to know is what's happening?'

'It could be the magnesium sulphate. Although it can stop premature labour, it can also have some worrying side effects,' Casey responded calmly. 'I've turned it off. Clara,' she addressed her patient, 'your lungs are filling up with fluid—that's why you're having so much trouble breathing, Dr Rhodes is coming directly.'

'I'm here.'

Never had she felt more helpless. She couldn't even respond to his endless questions, just struggled to get the air into her lungs as Timothy looked on anxiously. If ever she knew she had been wrong not to tell him, it was confirmed then.

It wasn't just the baby whose life was on the line but her own.

Her child, *their* child, could be left without a mother. Timothy should have been told and nothing would ever change that fact. She could only pray that one day he might understand.

'The baby,' Clara started, but Dr Rhodes just patted her hand.

'Things will start settling now, Clara,' he said confidently. 'We've given you some drugs to reverse the effects and your observations are settling. When things have calmed down I'll examine you—'

'The baby,' Clara gasped, and Dr Rhodes nodded gently, his tone almost patronising.

'It's you we're concerned with at the moment, Clara. The baby's doing just fine.'

But it wasn't what she was trying to say. Her agonised eyes swivelled to Timothy's as she struggled to make herself heard, struggled to make them understand.

'I think my waters just broke.'

It was on for young and old then. Emergency bells were pushed, monitors and IV poles swapped over for portable versions, the operating theatre being alerted, the safest place to deliver such a tiny infant in case Clara needed an emergency Caesarean. Dr

Rhodes examined her as Casey waited with her foot poised, ready to snap the brakes off the bed and move her.

'Fully dilated.' Dr Rhodes looked up at the nurse. 'Let's move.'

Move they did, but only as far as the door.

'It's coming,' Clara gasped.

'Don't push,' Casey said firmly, lifting the sheet, but as impassive as her voice was Clara knew what was happening, knew that this really was it. 'Let's get to the delivery room.'

It took just a matter of seconds. The earlier contractions had done their job, despite the best of modern medicine, and a tiny baby slipped into the world, coming, ready or not, as staff appeared from everywhere. The overhead chimes summoning the neonatal intensive care team to the delivery ward as Clara sobbed in Timothy's arms, scared to look yet terrified not to as her baby entered the world. There was no sound, no crying, but this wasn't the peaceful silence she had witnessed when Timothy had delivered Mary's baby. This was an awful void that seemed to go on for ever, just the briefest glimpse of her pale, limp babe, a glimmer of red hair visible as the tiny bundle was wrapped up and moved swiftly out.

Time was of the essence now.

'A little girl,' Clara said, as the NICU nurse dashed off.

'She's not crying.'

'They've taken her next door,' Casey said gently. 'They're all ready for her. They'll be giving her oxygen and getting her started.'

'Go with her,' Clara begged, as Timothy stood there torn, staring at Clara so pale, so very ill as his daughter's life also hung in the balance. 'Go with her,' Clara sobbed again as Casey pushed her back on the pillow and tightened the oxygen mask around her face.

'Take it easy, Clara. You're not well yourself.'

'Please, Timothy, go with her, stay with her. She's so tiny, she'll be so scared.'

It was the longest night of Clara's life.

Nurses popped in and out, giving her updates, the neonatologist came and gently guided Clara through her daughter's status, her treatment, her chances. And though the news was cautiously optimistic, nothing would calm Clara until she saw her daughter for herself, her anxiety mounting with each laboured breath until finally Casey gave her a sleeping tablet, insisting she get some rest.

'When can I see her?'

'When you're well enough' was the best Casey could offer. 'And the sooner you get some sleep, the sooner that will happen.'

It was the only reason she complied.

CHAPTER THIRTEEN

'HEY, you.'

Opening her eyes, for a second or two the world seemed OK, but it didn't last long.

There was Timothy smiling down at her, those green eyes gentle now, but Clara knew there had been tears and she dreaded what was coming next.

'Is she—?'

'She's beautiful,' Timothy said softly. 'Little stick arms and legs, and she's so tiny it terrifies me, Clara, but she's a fighter.' He picked up a handful of Polaroids and passed them to her. 'She's got your red hair.'

He stared at the picture a moment longer. 'The neonatologist thinks she's behaving as if she might even be twenty-nine weeks gestation.'

'Another thing I got wrong,' Clara mumbled.

'Another week's good,' Timothy said gently. 'And despite how you're feeling, you did really well, Clara. You hung in there long enough to give the steroids a chance to work. I'm so proud of you.'

She waited, waited for a 'but', waited for some recrimination, but it never came.

'I should have told you.'

'Yes,' he said slowly, 'you should have, but I know now that you tried.' Pulling an envelope out of his pocket, he laid it on the bed. 'This was in my pigeonhole in the doctors' mess. Why did you wait so long, Clara? Did you think I'd be angry or something, that I wouldn't stand by you?'

'I knew that you would stand by me,' Clara said cryptically. 'And that was the bit that worried me.' She looked up at his noncomprehending face. 'I don't want to have one of those marriages where people stay together for the sake of the children.'

'And that's what you think it would be?'

She didn't answer, just stared at her hands as he sat on the bed and let out a long weary sigh.

'Casey's called the porters and they're going to wheel you down to see our baby soon, but before we go there's one thing we have to agree on.' She looked up at his glittering eyes and knew that he was close to tears, but his voice was firm. 'Like it or not, I know now about the baby and whether you want me in her life is immaterial. I'm her father and nothing's going to change that fact.'

She gave a small nod but still she couldn't look at him.

'We need to talk, that much is clear. But not today. Today's about meeting our daughter, and if marriage isn't what you want, if a united front is the best we can manage for her, then it has to start here and now.'

A tiny frown puckered her brow, her red-rimmed eyes jerking up. 'You're the one who left, Timothy. You're the one who didn't want me.'

He didn't get a chance to answer as a midwife appeared with two porters hovering behind her and a huge smile on her face.

'Ready to meet your little lady?'

And even though there was so much to be said, so much that needed to be cleared up, Timothy was right. Now wasn't the time.

Someone else came first now.

'Now, you know what to expect,' the midwife checked as she kicked off the brakes. 'I explained about all the tubes—'

'I'm ready,' Clara broke in, wiping her face with backs of her hands, excited and scared all at once as the bed slid down the hall.

It took for ever to wash her hands, for the bell in the neonatal unit to be answered and the door to swing open, but finally she was being wheeled through and even though there must have been twenty cots, her eyes fixed only on one, tiny little tufts of red hair coming into focus as they pushed the bed up beside her.

'She's beautiful.' The staff had moved the equipment enough so the bed could be pushed alongside the incubator. Leaning over, Clara was able to put her hand in, and never had something felt so sweet, so soft, so pure. Tiny little fingers that curled around Clara's, her little chest moving up and down so fast, the soft down that covered her frowning forehead as her tiny closed eyelids moved rapidly.

'Mummy's here…' Clara whispered gently. And even though it felt strange to say it, to believe that after all the babies she'd delivered, all the newborns she'd held, this little one was actually hers. But the word came naturally from her lips, the gush of maternal love flowing so strong it made her catch her breath. Timothy's hand was on her shoulders, holding her tight as she gazed on and on, and even though she couldn't see him she could feel the love that emanated from him as he gazed upon his tiny daughter. 'Daddy's here, too,' she added, as Timothy's hand tightened on her shoulder. 'And we both love you so very much.'

'Have you chosen a name?' the nurse asked as Clara gazed on, overwhelmed, terrified, exhausted but utterly devoted, and it was Timothy who spoke, his voice thick with emotion, breaking every now and then.

'Not yet. We're just getting used to the fact she's here.'

'It's a lot to take in,' the nurse said gently, moving into the background but constantly present, the baby just too tiny to allow for anything else.

It *was* a lot to take in.

And for a few days their relationship, or what was left of it, was put on the back burner as they concentrated instead on their daughter. Feeling every needle, every tube and every grimace as she struggled to hold on, to stay with a world she had joined too early.

'I want to hold her.' Clara's dry eyes were no indicator of the pain behind her words and Timothy pulled her in closer, a cuddle all he could offer as the days ticked by into weeks.

'Tomorrow perhaps,' he said hopefully.

'They said that yesterday.' She could hear the mistrust in her voice, the gnawing panic that seemed to constantly snap at her, and she struggled to quash it.

They were living in a tiny flat attached to the neonatal unit. Although living might be a slight exaggeration—existing perhaps a more apt word.

Existing between visits to the unit, and long, long heart-stopping nights, praying for the phone not to ring…

Dying a bit inside when it did.

And no one could know, unless they had been there, the agony of those calls, the dash to the unit, washing your hands because you had to as staff rushed around behind those glass doors and struggled to get your baby through one more night. The lack of elation when the panic was over, just the cold fingers of fear as you wondered how much a tiny body could take, how long till this roller-coaster ride ended.

'They know what they're doing, Clara, you have to trust them.'

'I know.'

'And we have to start trusting each other.'

Clara jerked her eyes up and shook her head. She had known this day was coming, knew there was so much to sort out, but she simply couldn't deal with it now, her emotions so raw she simply couldn't take any more pain and be expected to function.

'We need to talk,' Timothy said softly. 'And if that's too hard, then I'll talk and you can listen.'

Wearily she nodded, bracing herself for the impact as she stared down at her hands.

'I can see why you don't want to get married, and if you'd bothered to talk to me about it you'd have found out that I actually agree with you. I had a miserable childhood, endless silences followed by endless rows followed my endless silences. It never ended and to this day it still goes on. My parents only stayed together ''for the sake of the children,'' and frankly I wish they hadn't bothered.' She heard the quotation marks around his words, heard the pain behind them, and tears filled her eyes for what he must have been through. 'The saddest part is, now that the children have finally grown up and left home, they're still stuck with each other, too bitter and jaded to pluck up the courage to leave. So you see, Clara, I do understand where you're coming from. I promised myself before I even knew what it really meant that if ever I married it would be the real thing, that if it wasn't what we both wanted then it wasn't worth doing.'

He knelt down beside her, taking her pale shaking hands in his. 'Even if we're not together, though, it doesn't mean I won't be there for you both, it doesn't mean I'm not going to be the best father I can be.'

He was right, she knew that deep down, knew there was no point in living together if he didn't really love her, but hearing him say it hurt like hell.

'I love you, Clara. I have since the day I met you.'

Startled, she looked up, her eyebrows furrowing as she begged a rewind on the previous conversation, her mouth opening to speak then closing again, sure she must somehow have misheard him, or more likely he was about to add a quick postscript: 'As a sister' perhaps or 'as the mother of my child'. But what he said next utterly floored her

'I just can't be second best.'

'You're not,' she croaked, then cleared her throat. 'You never have been.'

'Oh, Clara, you love Kell. Don't try and deny it now. Every time I mentioned his name, tried to find out how you were feeling, you shut me out, Matthew went missing, and who did you turn to? Everywhere I go he seems to be there. Hell, I'm surprised he wasn't the midwife on duty when you delivered.'

A very watery smile wobbled on her lips, but it changed midway and she started to cry.

'When Ross offered me the job I was so happy. I forgot we were supposed to be meeting at the pub and I raced over to the house and there were pictures all over the table, pictures of Kell, and I knew then I couldn't do it, couldn't keep pretending I was good enough, that I was what you wanted.'

'You *are* what I want,' Clara said. 'I couldn't talk about it because I thought I'd scare you off, and as for those pictures... He was getting married, Timothy. I was helping Shelly to put together some photos for Abby, and it didn't hurt a bit, not one single bit. My life was perfect from the day you came to Tennengarrah to the day you left. I love you, Timothy, I always have.'

'So why couldn't you tell me?' Timothy pushed. 'Why couldn't you just say it?'

'Because I didn't want you to feel sorry for me.' Screwing her eyes closed, she pulled her hands from his and covered her eyes, but he pulled them back down, cupping her face and forcing her to look.

'Who hurt you, Clara?' he rasped.

'No one hurt me,' she sobbed. 'Everyone's always been nice, but only because they had to be. I'm sick of being "poor Clara", I'm tired of people asking me for Christmas dinner just because they know I don't have a family, sick of the duty dances because they feel obliged—'

'Clara.' Timothy's voice broke in. 'They aren't doing those things out of a sense of duty. Your parents died fifteen years ago. Hell, where I come from the casseroles and visits end after a couple of weeks, but even allowing for Tennengarrah being a bit more neighbourly, I think fifteen years is pushing things.

'They love you, Clara. Not because of what happened but because of who you are. Good and kind and gentle. For the very same reasons that I love you.

'Love you,' he repeated, just so she could be absolutely sure she wasn't hearing things. 'I don't want to marry you out of duty. Life's too short for that. I want to be with you and only you, and I'm actually starting to believe that you might want to be with me. Can you see that now?'

She couldn't, not yet. He knew that, knew that her pain ran deep, and he held her close as he spoke.

'You didn't just lose your parents when you were fifteen,' he said softly. 'You lost that unconditional love that comes with it. Maybe I don't have the best mum and dad in the world but, as much as I rant and moan, deep down I know that they love me. I knew that when I was sixteen and had the worst acne in the world and no one would even come near me. I knew that when the first of many girls dumped me and even when I'd wasted three years studying for a degree I'll never use, as much as they berated me, they still loved me.

'You never had that, did you?' His eyes were brimming now. 'The confidence that being loved gives you?'

'Everyone was good...' she started, but then she gave in. Cried for all she had lost, all those lonely, lonely nights and the horrible, horrible feeling of never quite fitting in, never being quite good enough.

And he held her, held her and rocked her and loved her until finally, as the shadows on the wall lengthened, the world suddenly didn't seem such a lonely place, his strength, his touch giving her the confidence it took to say the three hardest words of her life.

'I love you.'

'And I love you, too.' Timothy kissed her salty cheeks, kissed her blonde eyelashes and held her tight. 'I got up yesterday and I hated the world without you. Hated the fact I get up now the second the alarm goes off because it's easier than lying in a bed without you, and I knew then that I had to talk to you. That's why I rang, not because you were pregnant—I didn't even know. And not because I felt obliged to, but because I love you and I don't think I can make it without you.' The ringing of the phone made them both jump, scared that somehow, because they hadn't been concentrating for a moment, hadn't been praying hard enough, their little girl might have slipped away.

Timothy got there first, listening intently as Clara hovered anxiously, wringing her hands as he replaced the receiver. 'What did they say? Is she all right?'

'Better than all right.' Timothy smiled. 'Our baby needs a cuddle.'

It was the sweetest moment of them all.

With shaking hands Clara undid her blouse as the nurse gently instructed. 'Your skin's the best blanket of all.'

And suddenly what she had yearned for, ached for was next to her now, the softest skin nuzzling in as the nurse wrapped a bunny rug around them, stepping back slightly as Timothy edged nearer, his camera ready, determined to capture this most precious moment. But in mid-shot he changed his mind and, putting the camera down, came over and held Clara, marvelling in the miracle they had created.

'I'll do the honours.' The nurse smiled, picking up the camera. 'One for the album.'

Clara didn't even look up as the photo was taken, her eyes never leaving her baby.

'Some memento of your holiday, huh?' Clara said softly as Timothy pulled them in closer.

'I wonder if I'll get her through customs.'

And then the joking stopped, the nerves, the shyness disappearing as their eyes locked above their tiny little red-headed babe.

'She needs a name,' Timothy said, his voice thick with emotion. 'We can't let them keep calling her Baby Watts. What was your mother's name?'

'Elizabeth,' Clara whispered. 'But everyone called her Beth.'

'Beth.' Timothy said the name slowly, his face breaking into a smile. 'Beth Morgan—it sounds nice, don't you think?'

Her eyes never left his, confidence, hope, love, tears all shining in her eyes.

'It sounds perfect.'

'She's going to be all right,' Timothy said softly, one large finger stroking the tiny pink cheek. 'More than all right, she's going to be just fine.'

And this time his optimism didn't irritate her, this time his blind faith didn't annoy her.

It was everything she needed.

'We're all going to fine,' he added softly.

EPILOGUE

'YOUR mum and dad would have been so proud of you.'

Bill's voice was gruff as he offered his arm, and Clara leant on it gratefully as he fussed over Beth with all the skill of a new grandfather, his daughter Martha's baby already a playmate for Beth.

'You look wonderful,' Eileen enthused, fiddling with Clara's dress as her heels sank into the dry red earth.

'So do you,' Clara whispered through her chattering teeth.

'At least I've managed to produce a bit of hair for the day.' Eileen grinned, fingering her fine, short hair. 'A bald maid of honour's not the best look.'

'I'm just glad you're here,' Clara said softly, the double meaning not wasted on Eileen as she smiled back fondly. And Eileen truly did look wonderful. Her thin face was filling out now, hope shining in her eyes at the beauty of a future she could glimpse now. They'd decided against a headdress of flowers for Eileen. She truly didn't need them. The wispy locks that framed her smiling face held all the hope of a meadow in springtime.

'Do you want me to take Beth for you?'

Clara shook her head. 'I want to walk up the aisle holding her.'

'They're all ready for you.' Hamo was walking towards her, unfamiliar in a dark suit, his hair for once neatly cut, the perfect groomsman for Tennengarrah's tiny church.

'Just give me a moment.'

Clara stood for a second gazing at the dusty town she loved, the barn all set up for this magical day, white ribbons adorning it, fairy-lights draped all ready for the biggest party Tennengarrah had ever witnessed. She gazed on the dry, hot land that was her home, knowing deep down that it was time to leave, to follow Timothy's dreams, to help him be all he was going to be.

'We'll be back,' Timothy had promised. 'When I'm a surgeon, we'll come back where we all belong.'

And they did belong, Clara knew that now.

They belonged to the endless red earth, to the family that was Tennengarrah, to the community that had embraced her, not because they'd had to but because they'd wanted to.

Love was never a duty.

But by Timothy's side was where she wanted to be now, where she was needed the most.

Walking towards him, she jumped slightly as the music thundered into life, as the whole of Tennengarrah turned towards her, smiling, taking every step with her as Timothy waited patiently.

Waited and watched as his family walked towards him.

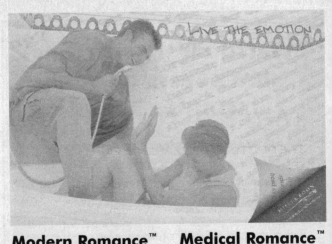
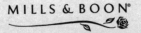

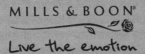

MILLS & BOON®

Live the emotion

Medical Romance™

THE DOCTOR'S UNEXPECTED FAMILY
by Lilian Darcy

The last thing Caroline Archer was looking for was
romance – so she was surprised to feel attraction for
her new colleague, Declan McCulloch. It was a
friendship that quickly developed into a passion – and
with that passion Caroline held a secret, a secret that
would keep Declan in Glenfallon for ever…

HIS PREGNANT GP *by Lucy Clark*

When Dr Jake Carson takes a position in a small town
practice in Australia, he expects his pace of life to
slow down. But when Jake discovers that the sexy,
single and pregnant Dr Rebekah Sanderson is his new
partner and housemate, he suddenly finds himself in at
the deep end!

THE ENGLISH DOCTOR'S BABY *by Sarah Morgan*

Alex Westerling is a brilliant doctor. He's also
never out of the celebrity magazines – he's an
aristocrat with a string of women lining up behind
him! That's until beautiful nurse Jenny Phillips turns
up on his doorstep, claiming that her late sister's
baby is *his* child!

On sale 7th May 2004

*Available at most branches of WHSmith, Tesco, Martins, Borders,
Eason, Sainsbury's and all good paperback bookshops.*

0404/03a

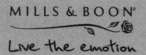